SUPERGRANNY

THE GREAT
COLLEGE CAPER

...aks out at
...-famous
...ow more
... field —
...amonds!
...elderly
...st of the

Supergranny Mysteries

Supergranny 1: The Mystery of the Shrunken Heads
ISBN 0-916761-10-X
Library Hardcover: ISBN 0-916761-11-8

Supergranny 2: The Case of the Riverboat Riverbelle
ISBN 0-916761-08-8
Library Hardcover: ISBN 0-916761-09-6

Supergranny 3: The Ghost of Heidelberg Castle
ISBN 0-916761-06-1
Library Hardcover: ISBN 0-916761-07-X

Supergranny 4: The Secret of Devil Mountain
ISBN 0-916761-04-5
Library Hardcover: ISBN 0-916761-05-3

Supergranny 5: The Character Who Came to Life
ISBN 0-916761-12-6
Library Hardcover: ISBN 0-916761-13-4

Supergranny 6: The Great College Caper
ISBN 0-916761-14-2
Library Hardcover: ISBN 0-916761-15-0

Buy Supergranny mysteries at your local bookstore, or ask the bookstore to order them. Or order them yourself with this coupon.

Holderby & Bierce, Publishing
P.O. Box 4296
Rock Island, IL 61201-4296

Please send the Supergranny mysteries checked above. Enclosed is my check or money order for $_____ ($2.95 for each paperback, $8.95 for each hardcover; plus $1.50 postage and handling per order.)

Name _____

Address _____

City _____ State _____ Zip _____

Allow 2 weeks for delivery.
Prices subject to change and offer to withdrawal without notice.

SUPERGRANNY

THE GREAT
COLLEGE CAPER

Beverly Hennen Van Hook

Holderby & Bierce

Published by Holderby & Bierce, P.O. Box 4296,
Rock Island, IL 61201-4296

Andrea Nelken, editor

Paperback. ISBN 0-916761-14-2
Library Hardcover. ISBN 0-916761-15-0

SUMMARY: Supergranny gives the Poindexter kids and her readers a
taste of college life when she helps a handsome, elderly history professor
and his llama, Leonard, search for stolen diamonds. Sixth in the series
about a gray-haired detective who drives a red Ferrari and fights crime.

Holderby & Bierce, October, 1991

Printed in the U.S.A.

To Katie, Jamie, and Ohio University

Max was selling burritos at the Burrito Buggy when we got to the Ohio Keptheart University campus. It was a sunny fall afternoon and the Buggy, a mini-restaurant on wheels, was mobbed by hungry college students.

We finally made it to the front of the mob.

Max, Supergranny's great-nephew, was so glad to see her he practically fell out of his counter window. Then he started pushing burritos, pop and chips at us, which was fine with me because we hadn't eaten a thing since breakfast at our Indiana motel 250 miles back.

"I told you these are the best burritos in the Midwest," Supergranny said, taking a humongous bite.

"And the messiest," Max added.

Max works at the Burrito Buggy to help pay for

college. We'd driven in from Illinois to spend Homecoming weekend with him.

"It will be a chance for the kids to see what college is really like," Supergranny told our parents when she invited my older sister, Angela, my younger sister, Vannie, and me on the 520-mile trip.

Supergranny, as you may know, is our neighbor across the ravine. Her real name is Sadie Geraldine Oglepop, but we call her "Supergranny" because she's in her seventies, drives a Ferrari and solves crimes. And has a state-of-the-art mini-robot and a secret room behind her fireplace. And flies a Gulfstream jet. Just for starters.

Anyway, it was our school's fall break and our parents said OK.

"It will be so educational for the children," Mom said.

"And so quiet and peaceful for us at home," Dad added.

As always, Supergranny had also brought along our bashful Old English sheepdog, Shackleford, and her mini-robot, Chesterton.

Max turned the buggy over to his sub and led us to a brick wall beside a statue of ol' Caleb Keptheart, the founder of OKU. We sat down on the wall and seriously attacked our burritos while he went over plans for the weekend.

"You can stay in my room at the dormitory, Joshua," he said to me. Supergranny, Angela and Vannie would stay with Max's friend, Jeannie, in another part of the dorm.

"But I'm sorry to say dogs aren't allowed in the

dorm," Max said.

At that, Shackleford tilted her head to the right, stared at Max and tried to look cute.

"She thinks you're going to say 'kennel' as in 'Let's take her to the kennel'," Angela explained, "so she's trying to look cute."

"She thinks we won't take her to the kennel if she looks cute," Vannie added.

Shackleford tilted her head to the left and tried to look cuter.

Max laughed.

"No kennel," Max said, laughing. "Dreamwhopper's."

Shackleford wagged her rear happily. (She doesn't have a tail, so she wags her rear.) She must have figured whatever "Dreamwhopper's" was, it was better than "kennel."

"Dr. Delano Dreamwhopper, my history professor, has invited Shackleford and Chesterton to stay at his farm on the outskirts of town," Max explained. "You'll be meeting him soon. I got permission to bring you to class."

"Some people say he's a little odd, but he's really a great guy. And what a farm! Aunt Sadie, you're going to love it. You're in for a big surprise."

He got that right! But, never suspecting HOW right, we just grinned and chewed, trying to keep salsa from squirting out of our burritos, running down our arms and flooding our shoes.

We were in for a supermongo big surprise, all right. *And so was Max.*

       *   *   *   *

3

Odd or not, Dr. Dreamwhopper sure is a popular professor, and his 2 p.m. class, "Recent U.S. History," was already crammed when we got there.

Max managed to find five desks in the back.

"JUST ONCE, I wish we could WALK into a room and SIT without uproar," Angela muttered as we made our way to the back of the room.

This time, Chesterton caused the uproar.

Supergranny and Chesterton ADORE lectures and go to them all the time at home. "Why Mangrove Trees Grow on Stilts," "How Lightning Bugs Light: The Secret of Bioluminescence," — you name the lecture, they hit it. Chesterton records every word, then Supergranny listens to the tapes through earphones while she gardens or loads the dishwasher. It helps her remember the major points.

As soon as we walked into the room, Chesterton sensed "lecture" and began hopping, beeping and blinking his "Push Record" button.

It was embarrassing.

The whole crammed-full room of college students went goofy, laughing and pointing and shouting, "Is that a robot?" "Where can I buy one?" "Is that a dog?" "Do they allow dogs in here?" "Do you mind if I ask how much that robot cost?"

But at least they were friendly, especially one extre-e-emely good-looking woman student who Max introduced as his friend, Jeannie.

Supergranny plopped Chesterton on her desk, and Vannie punched his "Record" button to keep him busy, while Shackleford, who isn't quite so fond of lectures, crawled under my desk, put her head on her paws and pretended to sleep.

And just in time. A tall, sixtyish-looking man strode into the room.

"Pretty silver hair," Vannie whispered.

"Nice tan," Angela whispered.

"Nice-looking," Supergranny whispered.

Jeannie and Max grinned. "He's anxious to meet you, Aunt Sadie," Max said. "He has followed your cases for years."

"He wants to talk with you about a crime he's researching," Jeannie added.

Professor Dreamwhopper placed a worn, black, loose-leaf notebook on a lectern, glanced around the room and smiled.

My first college class was about to begin.

2

I'm no expert on college, since that was my first college class, but I think ol' Dreamwhopper is one terrific professor.

After all, how often do college students *applaud* a professor at the end of a class?

Hardly ever, according to Max.

"In fact, Dreamwhopper is the only professor I've ever heard applauded," Max said. "You should have been here last week. He got a standing ovation."

"A standing what?" Vannie asked.

"Ovation," Jeannie explained. "Where the audience STANDS UP to applaud."

After the class, we'd dumped our stuff at the dorm and were driving on a curvy, two-lane road out to the Dreamwhopper farm.

Jeannie, Max, Vannie and I led in Jeannie's car.

Supergranny and the others followed in the Ferrari.

It was a golden drive. Tangled gold trees, weeds and flowers lined the road, shimmering gold leaves tossed in the wind, gold sunlight warmed our faces through the windows.

"I can see why Dreamwhopper doesn't mind this drive every day," Jeannie said. "It's enchanting ... which makes the whole thing even more sad."

She frowned, gunning the car to pass a coal truck wheezing its way up a hill.

"What do you mean 'sad'?" Vannie asked.

"Can you keep a secret?" Max asked.

Vannie and I nodded.

"Are you sure?"

"Sure," I said.

"Absolutely," Vannie said.

I stifled a snort. Vannie keeps secrets like screens keep back air. But I was too curious myself to warn them.

"He's about to get canned from the university," Max said. "Let go. Fired."

That was a surprise. Why would OKU fire such a popular teacher? Such a nice guy?

"Don't they think he's any good?" Vannie asked.

"Oh, they know he's good," Max said. "They don't have anything against his teaching."

"Then what?" I asked.

"It's ... other things," Max said slowly. "His research. Some people are angry about his research."

"And the farm," Jeannie added. "People think it's odd. I mean they don't mind professors being a *little*

7

odd, that's OK. Adds color. Makes college more interesting. But they think he overdoes it."

I replayed my first impression of Dreamwhopper: Good looking. Silver hair. Knew his subject. Polite. Friendly. Popular. What's so odd about him? You see odder people every day, I thought. Much odder.

Then I met Leonard the Llama.

*   *   *   *

Leonard was waiting on the porch with Dr. Dreamwhopper as we pulled into the gravel drive.

He was as big as a small horse and totally hairy and he stood so still at first I thought he was stuffed. At least, I hoped he was stuffed.

"Er, that thing on the porch," Vannie said, "is it real?"

"Er, is that a *llama*?" I asked.

"Er, that thing's stuffed, isn't it?" Vannie asked.

Max and Jeannie didn't hear us. They were already out of the car and heading toward the porch, but Vannie and I hadn't budged from the back seat.

I looked out the rear window. They weren't tripping all over themselves hopping out of the Ferrari, either.

Shackleford took one horrified look at the porch and started barking her head off. I'm not sure what she was barking, but I *think* it was "TAKE ME TO THE KENNEL" and I *know* it was anti-llama.

The thing on the porch turned its head for a better look at Shackleford.

"Uh-oh, it moves," Vannie said.

"DON'T MIND LEONARD," Dreamwhopper

8

shouted from the porch. "HE'S PERFECTLY SAFE."

Meanwhile, Max was sort of bowing to the thing, and it was — yech!—*kissing Jeannie's cheek*.

Supergranny's door opened in the Ferrari. She got out, carrying Chesterton.

Angela's door opened. She got out, yanking Shackleford's leash. Shackleford's head and front paws skidded onto the gravel. Angela gave another mighty yank. Shackleford's rear half followed.

I opened my door.

Vannie opened her door.

We joined the cozy little group on the porch.

"Do come in," Dreamwhopper was saying. "I'm so glad you could fit the farm into your busy weekend. And we're DELIGHTED that Chesterton and Shackleford can stay with us. Leonard LOVES company."

Meanwhile all of us — Leonard included — moved inside.

The farmhouse living room was lined with floor-to-ceiling bookcases and had a stone fireplace big enough for a llama to stand up in.

I was glad to see it was neat and clean and smelled like Lemon Pledge. That might sound snobbish, but I'd never seen a house with a llama living in it before, and I half expected stench and turmoil. The truth is, it was five times neater than my room at home and fifty times neater than Vannie's.

We'd met Dreamwhopper briefly after class, so we could bypass getting introduced to him and get right down to meeting Leonard.

"I've had him since I moved in five years ago,"

Dreamwhopper explained. "Some people up the road moved out and left poor Leonard to fend for himself. I'd gotten used to llamas when I was doing research in the Andes mountains, so I figured, why not? Llamas are terrific pets, don't you know?"

"Yes, but aren't they on the stubborn side?" Angela asked. "I did a report on llamas for school; they're supposed to be stubborn, aren't they?"

(Angela, as you may know, has done a report on every subject in the world and gotten at least an A- on all of them.)

Dreamwhopper laughed. "They're almost as stubborn as people," he said.

"Of course, they're very useful," Angela went on, determined to give the whole danged report if nobody stopped her. "South American Indians use them to carry supplies across the mountains. And make clothes from their wool. And eat them."

I thought that last remark might offend Leonard, but he didn't seem to mind. He just stood by the fireplace, looking dignified. He was so quiet, Shackleford got up the courage to crawl out from under Angela's chair, look straight at Leonard and sniff.

"And they're not picky eaters," Angela went on. "Just horse-feed pellets and some grass now and then."

"Angela, you're absolutely right," Dreamwhopper said.

"And if they have to, they can go for days without water," Angela went on.

Luckily, Dr. Dreamwhopper saved us from any more llama lore. "Not to change the subject, but I have a favor to ask Ms. Oglepop," he said.

The favor was he invited Supergranny to stay for dinner and didn't invite us. We'd eat back at campus with Max, then Supergranny and Dreamwhopper would drive his Jeep to town later and meet us at the campus Comedy Club.

Max was all for it, because it meant he got to drive the Ferrari back to campus. Supergranny was all for it, too, although for the life of me I couldn't figure out why she'd drive 520 miles to wind up eating spaghetti with a guy and a llama.

"I've stumbled onto something very mysterious in a research project I'm working on, and I'd like to discuss it with you," Dreamwhopper told her.

Just then we noticed the noise. It was coming from Leonard, who was still standing by the fireplace looking dignified.

"Hmmmmmmmmmmm," went Leonard.

Shackleford retreated under Angela's chair.

"Hmmmmmmmmmm," went Leonard.

"He's humming," Vannie said. "Leonard's humming."

"Oh, that just means he has to go out," Dreamwhopper said. "Joshua, would you let him out the back door, please?"

I walked into the kitchen and held open the door to the fenced-in back yard. I hoped he wasn't in a hurry. I hadn't planned to spend my first day at college getting trampled by a llama on his way to the bathroom.

No sweat. Totally cool Leonard strolled past, still humming and looking dignified.

11

3

The good news about Max's dormitory room is its great view of the South Green.

The bad news is that it's as small as an elevator and it's crammed with a twin bed, desk, computer, mini-refrigerator, TV, stereo system, lamps, a tennis racket, golf clubs, and 148 stacks of books, file folders, newspapers and magazines.

Even the bed was covered. A six-foot Charlie Chaplin poster that had just fallen off the wall was stretched out on it.

I finally managed to stuff my sleeping bag in the closet and slam the door before my bag could explode back out at me. Then I unpacked a few things and stacked them on the stereo speaker.

Max still wasn't back from helping Angela and

Vannie carry their stuff to Jeannie's room, so I picked up the poster and sat down on the bed to wait.

Two windows met at a corner by the bed. I moved back in the corner, holding the Charlie Chaplin poster over me like a tent to keep it from wrinkling.

There was college life down below.

South Green is like a little city of college students. It has blocks and blocks of five-story, red brick dorms with white trim. No cars are allowed on the streets, which are lined with red and gold maple trees.

Up the hill to the left, you can barely see the main campus classroom buildings. The rest of South Green is ringed by a golf course and playing fields framed by distant hills.

I sat quietly in my Charlie Chaplin tent, watching the show below.

Eight thousand college students live on South Green, and it looked like most of them were down there. Thousands poured down the hill from class with book bags slung over their shoulders. Hundreds played Frisbee and football on the lawns. Dozens grouped in clumps on brick walls and porches, laughing and talking. "Jungle Fever" by Stevie Wonder boomed from a window in the next dorm. A couple leaned against a doorway, hugging and kissing.

I pictured myself as a college student in a few years.

There I was in jeans and an OKU sweatshirt with a book bag over one shoulder. I was wearing wire-rimmed circle glasses. I looked totally smart. I looked totally cool. A gorgeous girl was walking beside me. She was smiling.

I had just decided that OKU was definitely the college

for me when I realized someone else was in the room.

Someone had closed the door softly and switched on Max's computer.

Max, I thought, pulling down the poster. But before I could say "Max" I realized it *wasn't* Max.

A stranger wearing a green, hooded sweatshirt was sitting at Max's computer. Probably one of Max's friends who didn't realize somebody was under the poster. He'd probably think I was a nutcake to be sitting under a Charlie Chaplin poster.

What should I do?

Cough?

Say, "Hi, I'm visiting from Illinois."?

Before I could decide, the guy did something weird.

He stopped scanning through the computer directory and looked toward the door as though he'd heard a noise in the hall. Quickly, he switched off the computer, grabbed a magazine and leaned back in the chair.

I canceled coughing. I canceled speaking. Something was wrong with this picture.

Nothing happened.

Hooded Sweatshirt tiptoed to the door, leaned against it and listened, never looking my way.

Nothing happened.

After a few seconds, he sat back down at the computer, switched it on and quickly jotted notes in a small brown book he pulled from his pocket.

I'm no expert on typical dorm life, but don't tell me this was it. Something was *definitely* wrong with this picture.

I inched the poster back over my face.

After what seemed like forty years, but was probably five minutes, I heard him switch off the computer and close the door.

Was he gone?

Or was it a trick?

Was he standing there waiting to have a nice belly laugh when the nutcake popped out of the Charlie Chaplin poster?

I started counting to twenty by thousands ... one thousand, two thousand, three thousand....

At eighteen thousand I couldn't stand it any longer. I dropped the poster three inches.

The room was empty.

Then it was full again as Vannie, Angela, Max and Jeannie came roaring back.

"Isn't it fabulous, Joshua?" Angela was saying. "You should *see* Jeannie's room. It's in the same mod but on the other side of the TV room." (The dorm was divided into modules, and Max's mod was 4A, which was all guys. Jeannie's all-girl mod on the same floor was 4B.)

"Jeannie's roommate is from Namibia in Africa, and she's a part-time model and when we get back to the dorm tonight, she's going to cornrow my hair," Vannie said.

"Great," I said. "Max —"

"She says I have beautiful hair," Vannie bragged.

"Great," I said. "Max —"

"Grab your jacket, Josh," Max interrupted. "We just have time to catch supper at Scum."

Before I had a chance to say "MAX, A STRANGE

15

GUY IN A HOODED SWEATSHIRT SNEAKED INTO YOUR ROOM AND COPIED SOMETHING FROM YOUR COMPUTER," we were down the stairs and on our way to Dascumb Dining Hall, which everybody calls "Scum."

Swarms of college students were everywhere.

"A STRANGE GUY IN A HOODED SWEATSHIRT SNEAKED INTO YOUR ROOM AND COPIED SOMETHING FROM YOUR COMPUTER" isn't something you blurt out in the middle of a swarm.

I'll wait until we get to Scum, I thought. *Then I'll sit next to Max and tell him quietly, man to man, while we eat.*

I thought wrong.

Because before I could put my tray down beside Max, a muscular blond guy plunked his tray between us.

"Yo, Max, who are the Munchkins?"

He was talking about us. He was calling us Munchkins.

Max smiled. "Yo, Ben, meet my friends from Illinois – Angela, Joshua and Vannie. They live next door to my Aunt Sadie."

"This is Ben," Max said to us, "a starting running back for the Ohio Keptheart Kangaroos. You'll see him in the game tomorrow. Ask him anything, but don't ask him about OK's 0-3 record this year. Or about their 2-7 record last year, or —"

"Cap it, Maxie, tomorrow's a new day. Glad to meet you," Ben said to us with a big grin.

He was Max's best friend from Dayton, Ohio, he was majoring in business and he was so friendly I could have forgiven him for calling us Munchkins – except for one thing.

He was wearing a green, hooded sweatshirt.

As soon as we finished what was *supposed* to be roast beef, mashed potatoes, green beans and canned pears, we were off to the Comedy Club. (Actually, Scum's roast beef isn't as bad as I'd heard, but you're supposed to knock dorm food, so I'm practicing.)

"We have seven minutes to get there. Run fast and practice laughing," Max said as we sent our trays back to the kitchen on Scum's movable belt.

"Jeannie is doing her act and needs laugh support. I know. I helped write it."

Running fast and laughing hard gives me chest pains, so I just focused on running. I'd worry about laughing later. And telling Max about Hooded Sweatshirt.

Ben had left us right after dinner to meet his

girlfriend at the library.

Was he Hooded Sweatshirt?

Why hadn't he mentioned it to Max at supper? Something like, "Yo, Max, I borrowed some stuff off your computer," or whatever?

On the other hand, there were probably 5,000 hooded sweatshirts on campus. Why suspect Ben?

After all, except for calling us "Munchkins," Ben seemed like a nice guy. And he was Max's best friend.

I hoped it hadn't been Ben. What a nerd I was to sit there with a poster over my head. Why hadn't I said something?

By the time we got to the Comedy Club, I was sick of thinking about the whole thing. I was also about to collapse. OKU is a hilly campus. Every place you go is down one hill and up and down two more.

On second thought, maybe I *wouldn't* go to OKU. Maybe I'd look for a *flat* college.

*   *   *   *

The Comedy Club, which is in a small campus theater, was packed with college students. We got to our seats just as the curtain rose. Supergranny and Dreamwhopper's seats were empty.

"They must be running late," Max whispered. "They'll probably sit in the back."

Jeannie stood center stage, wearing a purple satin dress and a little crown that glittered like diamonds.

She looked beautiful and elegant, except that she was also wearing hiking boots and carrying a megaphone and a pooper scooper.

She clomped to the front of the stage in the hiking

boots. CLOMP, CLOMP, CLOMP, CLOMP.

Everybody laughed.

Her act was a dog obedience class where totally ritzy people brought their dogs to learn how to behave. She was the teacher, with the accent of a snooty British countess and the heart of a military dictator.

The audience was the class. We all had to stand up and pretend we had a dog on a leash.

Then she introduced the demonstration dogs on stage: Dinky, Suds, Bartholomew and Chuck.

They were all imaginary and each had its own musical sounds to go with its name.

To her right was Dinky the Doberman. As she introduced him, a flute trilled offstage. We all had to applaud Dinky without letting go of our leash.

Suds was a St. Bernard. Her music was a few whiny violin notes.

Bartholomew the Basset's music was four slow notes on a bassoon that sounded like Bar   Thol   O   Mew in a deep, tired voice.

Bar Thol O Mew, went the bassoon's four notes again.

Bar   Thol   O   O   O   O — Uh - oh. The bassoon was stuck on the third note.

"Bartholomew, get off your ear," Jeannie barked.

Everybody laughed. Bartholomew was stuck; he'd stepped on one of his droopy, giant ears.

Last was Chuck the   Chihuahua, whose music was one BOOM of a bass drum. Chuck might be tiny, but he was a VERY macho chihuahua. It was clear from the start he was trouble.

Jeannie began the lesson by showing us how to hold the leash. Then she showed us how to walk with our dog near our left heel, how to yank the leash when the dog did something asinine like lunge for a biker, and how to tug the leash and tap the dog's rump at the same time to make it sit.

"Heel!" she barked. We all walked in place, pretending we were walking our dogs in a circle while the music played.

The flute trilled. The violin whined. The bassoon droned. The drum boomed. I could picture Dinky, Suds, Bartholomew and Chuck up on stage marching in a circle.

The flute trilled. The violin whined. The bassoon droned. The drum went BOOM, BOOM, BOOM.

Uh-oh. Chuck was going too fast.

BOOM, BOOM, BOOM, BOOM, BOOM.

The flute trilled. The drum boomed. The violin whined, the drum boomed, the bassoon droned, the drum boomed.

Uh-oh! CHUCK WAS PASSING EVERYONE!

Jeannie spun in circles, shrieking at Chuck through her megaphone.

BOOMBOOMBOOM! Chuck didn't pay the slightest attention.

Jeannie was going berserk, screeching at Chuck and flailing the pooper scooper in his direction. In between, she was commanding us: "SIT!" "HEEL!" "SIT!" "HEEL!"

We marched in place, we yanked the leash, we swatted our imaginary dog on the rump. We got mixed up. Some people heeled when they were

21

supposed to sit. Some people swatted when they were supposed to heel.

Flute drum violin drum bassoon drumdrumdrum.

Everybody pictured the tiny chihuahua TEARING around the stage THROUGH the legs of Dinky the Doberman OVER the back of Suds the St. Bernard. While ol' Bar Thol O Mew plodded along, tripping on his ears.

"HIT! SEEL! HIT! SEEL!" screamed Jeannie, getting confused.

People broke into the aisles, heeling and sitting and patting each other's dogs and pretending to step in dog poop.

Flutedrumviolindrumbassoondrumdrumdrum went the music.

"GRAB THAT CHIHUAHUAAAA!" Jeannie shrieked, pointing the pooper scooper down the center aisle.

Uh-oh! Chuck had bolted.

People lunged for the imaginary chihuahua and missed; they climbed over the back of seats after him; they jumped as he darted between their legs.

"HE'S COMING OUR WAY!" Max yelled, springing into the aisle. Angela, Vannie and I crowded around him, forming a human fence.

Chuck raced straight toward me. I slammed to my knees to stop him. Too late! Vannie and Angela dived for him, but he slipped from their grasp.

MAX GOT HIM!

He held imaginary Chuck above his head as everybody cheered.

Max grimaced in pain. "CHUCK BIT ME!"

The drum rolled; the curtain fell. Everybody was laughing and applauding and giving imaginary biscuits to their imaginary dogs.

Jeannie's act was a hit, and Mom was right. College *is* very educational.

5

After the show we and about five hundred students, professors and friends crowded backstage to congratulate Jeannie. Everybody was hugging, laughing and shouting, and in the excitement we didn't realize something was wrong until Jeannie sat down to take off her stage makeup.

"Wait a minute," Vannie said. "Where's Supergranny?"

We looked around the noisy room.

No Supergranny. No Dreamwhopper.

"Maybe they're waiting out front," Angela said.

Max and Jeannie frowned.

"But Dr. Dreamwhopper *always* comes backstage when one of his students performs," Jeannie said. "He's his students' No. 1 Fan."

"And Supergranny *always* meets us on time. *Always*," Angela said, looking worried.

Max went out front to look anyway.

No Supergranny. No Dreamwhopper.

"Maybe they had car trouble and are stuck at the farm," Max said. "Lend me a quarter."

Angela handed him a quarter and he called the farm from the pay phone backstage.

No answer.

"I don't like it," Max said grimly.

Jeannie stared at him. "You don't suppose ... I mean those break-ins ... you don't suppose someone actually ..." her voice trailed off.

"What break-ins?" Angela asked.

"Someone actually what?" Vannie asked.

Jeannie and Max ignored them. They frowned harder.

"We're going out there," Max said. "Josh, come with me to get the Ferrari. Angela and Vannie, help Jeannie get her stuff together."

Seven minutes later, we picked them up at the Comedy Club alley door. Jeannie tossed her tote with her long dress and fake diamond tiara in the trunk, and we were off.

"We can return the tiara to the wardrobe room tomorrow," she said. "Finding Supergranny and Dr. Dreamwhopper is more important."

*   *   *   *

"Great. Fog. Just what we need — **x*@@ fog," Max grumbled as he drove the Ferrari slowly along the twisting country road.

25

It was the kind of fog where you peer through the bottom of the windshield searching for the center line. The kind where the world seems to end in a gray wall one foot in front of your car hood. The kind where you wish you could forget the steep dropoffs you remember beside the road.

I'm talking spooky, scary, Halloweeny fog.

While Max grumbled about the fog, Jeannie filled us in on Dr. Dreamwhopper's Caleb Keptheart problem.

Old Caleb Keptheart was the founding father of Ohio Keptheart University.

"He turned up here in 1832, wearing a white silk suit, lizard boots, and a Panama hat and riding a palomino stallion called Forever Gold. He spoke with an English accent and was as rich as Bill Cosby and as handsome as Tom Cruise.

"Some said he was the rotten apple of a wealthy English family. Others said he'd won his money in a card game or robbed a diamond mine. But everybody agreed he danced, quoted Shakespeare and sat a horse better than anybody in the county.

"In 1840 he married a young actress who was a descendant of Daniel Boone. He idolized her and always called her "Queen Anne" after her most famous role. She gave up her stage career, but encouraged theater at the college and even starred in some campus plays. They had one child, a son, born in 1849.

"By the time Caleb died at the age of ninety-three he owned 3,000 acres. In the meantime he had founded the university, built the town, designed the courthouse, served six terms in the Ohio legislature,

26

and taken Charles Dickens and Mark Twain to lunch — at different times, of course.

"By then most folks had forgotten his shadowy past and considered him a patron saint or *at least* as respectable as a roomful of Supreme Court justices. Since then, his reputation has been polished, buffed and varnished more each year.

"So you can see why so many people are mad at Dr. Dreamwhopper," she said.

"No," I said, holding my breath as the center line disappeared in a wave of fog. "I can't," I said, breathing again as it surfaced.

"Me, either," Vannie said.

"I don't get the connection," Angela said.

"His *research*," Jeannie said patiently. "Dr. Dreamwhopper began doing a lot of research on Keptheart after he moved to the farm. It was the last Keptheart holding. Caleb's son died there in 1927. He didn't have children, so the farm was sold.

"Dr. Dreamwhopper has uncovered evidence that Caleb *wasn't* the saint everybody thinks he was."

"Hallelujah," Max interrupted. "We made it!"

We inched up Dreamwhopper's gravel drive and parked by the barn.

"But what did he do?" Vannie asked, returning to the Keptheart saga.

"Dreamwhopper's not sure yet," Max said, turning off the ignition. "But there's evidence that he really *did* rob a diamond mine *and hid some of the loot out here at the farm.*"

6

The barnyard was so foggy we couldn't see the bats screeching above our heads. We couldn't even see the rope hanging from the hayloft. But we could hear it.

Slap, slap, slap went the rope against the barn.

Slap, slap, slap, it went as we felt our way along the fence to the farmhouse gate.

The farmhouse itself stood on a small patch of hill and seemed to float above the fog like a ship at sea. It was dark. It looked deserted. It hummed.

Hummmmmmmm went the deserted farmhouse.

"LEONARD!" Vannie yelled. "He's in there and needs to go out!"

The sound of her voice provoked a riot of beeping and barking.

"CHESTERTON AND SHACKLEFORD!" Angela yelled.

We raced up the steps to the front door, and Max whipped out his key.

Leonard, Shackleford and Chesterton bounded out.

I was afraid Leonard would bolt like Chuck the imaginary Chihuahua, but he had only one thing on his mind. He had to go and he had to go BAD.

Afterward he just hung around the porch, watching Shackleford and Chesterton go bonkers.

Chesterton has had conniption fits before, but THIS was a masterpiece. He beeped, he whirred, he blinked. And he jumped — I kid you not — nine inches off the ground. And he's only as tall as a loaf of bread to begin with.

Meanwhile, Shackleford was making great FLYING leaps off the end of the porch, rushing to the fence, barking like a maniac, then BOUNDING back onto the porch to do it again.

My heart turned cold as frozen yogurt.

I knew darned well what they were trying to say.

"They're trying to tell us Supergranny is in trouble," Angela said soberly.

I knew in my frozen-yogurt heart she was right.

Vannie started to sniffle.

"No crying now, Vannie. We've got to think," Angela said.

That might sound mean, but she put her arm around Vannie as she said it. And this *wasn't* any time for tears.

We've come up against a lot with Supergranny — shrunken-head thieves, the notorious Twittle Twins, a haunted castle scam, Balkhastani thugs, a murderer who seemed to step out of a book. But we'd never been in a fix like this. Normally, if you call that stuff normal, Supergranny was with us, calling the shots.

This was different.

Here *we* were.

But where was she?

*　　　　　*　　　　　*　　　　　*

"How about Plan 239 G?" Angela asked quietly.

"Or 431 Z5," I suggested.

"I always like 101 AB," Vannie said.

"Good idea, Vannie, but 101 AB works better in daylight," Angela said, trying to be agreeable. "Actually, Joshua has a point. Maybe we should use Base Plan 239 but add variation Z5 as you suggested."

I still thought 431 Z5 was best, but after all, she was TRYING to lead without bossing, so why waste time arguing?

"Check," I said. "Plan 239 Z5."

"Check," Vannie said.

"Say what?" asked Max.

"It's a plan Supergranny taught us," I said quickly. "For situations like this."

"It means divide up, search the house, and signal if you find anything," Angela said.

"Then we meet here in two minutes," Vannie said.

"And follow Chesterton and Shackleford," I said.

"And we'll need flashlights from the Ferrari for that," Angela said.

"I'll get the flashlights," Max said. "Jeannie, are you in?"

"Plan 239 Z5 sounds fine to me," Jeannie replied quietly.

We divided into three teams.

Team 1 (Jeannie and Vannie) took the main floor.

Team 2 (Angela and Shackleford) took the upstairs.

Team 3 (Chesterton and I) took the basement.

Leonard stood sentry by the door, and Max went for the flashlights.

We raced into the house, switching on every light we could find. Fortunately, there was one at the top of the basement stairs. I was a little squeamish about the basement, but Chesterton was too upset to be scared of anything. He bounced down the stairs ahead of me, whirring and beeping and flashing as if to say, "I TOLD you, LUNKHEAD, there's nothing DOWN here."

In two minutes we were back on the porch.

Jeannie and Vannie hadn't found anything except the kitchen table set for two and a pot of spaghetti sauce simmering on the stove.

Angela and Shackleford hadn't found anything except the phone off the hook.

"Supergranny and Dr. Dreamwhopper didn't even have time to eat," Angela said grimly.

At that, Shackleford bounded over the porch railing, scrambled to her feet, took a big running start and sailed over the fence.

Chesterton scooted under the fence after her.

Max tossed each of us a flashlight, and we were after them.

Over the fence and into the murky woods.

31

7

Max led with Leonard on a rope.

The rest of us followed single file along a steep, narrow trail. Trees, brambles, weeds, hill and sky above to the left. Fog below to the right.

Meanwhile, Shackleford and Chesterton raced ahead. We couldn't see them, so we just followed the sounds of their barking, beeping and general racket.

Of course, Plan 239 Z5 calls for absolute quiet, but shutting them up was hopeless. Somebody had Supergranny and they were MAD. I just hoped our enemy — he, she, it or they — wasn't hiding on the trail, waiting to ambush us. Because thanks to Shackleford and Chesterton, we sure didn't have surprise on our side.

"Think positive," I told myself. "Maybe the racket

will scare off the enemy."

"HAH!" myself said back, not buying it. "And maybe Leonard can fly!"

Speaking of Leonard, he wasn't exactly helping.

You may have heard that llamas are surefooted, and they are. My ankles were already complaining about trying to keep my feet moving ALONG the hill instead of sliding DOWN it, while ahead of me old Leonard strolled along, calm as pudding.

Now and then he even stopped to eat grass.

He did NOT seem to grasp that this was a crisis.

WHO or WHAT had enticed Supergranny and Dreamwhopper away from their spaghetti?

WHO or WHAT had kept them from meeting us at the Comedy Club?

WHO or WHAT had knocked the phone off the hook?

WHO or WHAT was hiding along this trail?

NONE of these burning questions fazed Leonard. All he seemed to think about was looking dignified and eating the dratted grass.

After his third snack, Jeannie got testy.

"For Pete's sake, Max, move that llama," she whispered loudly.

"I can't," Max whispered back. "You can't rush a llama. He'll get offended and won't go ANYWHERE."

"Offended!" Jeannie fumed, forgetting all about Plan 239 Z5's rule of silence. "We're stuck out here in the middle of the night IN fog while heaven knows WHAT has happened to your Aunt Sadie and Dr. Dreamwhopper, and you're worried about OFFENDING a llama."

"Hey, Babe, I'm doing the best I can," Max hissed back. "If you're such a hotshot llama leader, come up here and lead him yourself."

"Oh, grow up!" Jeannie hissed back.

I thought they were going to break up over a llama right there in the fog, but, luckily, Leonard moved out, just in time.

The trail rounded a boulder and started straight down into a hollow.

Down, down, down we went, ducking tree limbs and climbing over underbrush. Jeannie, Angela and Vannie kept crashing into me, making me fall down sideways to keep from crashing into Leonard. (I didn't know his views on getting crashed into from behind, and I didn't want to find out.)

At last we caught up with our fearless leaders. Chesterton was whipping around a small clearing, making a racket you could hear all the way to West Virginia, while Shackleford was digging frantically at the side of a hill.

Suddenly she stopped digging.

Her ears perked. Chesterton stopped beeping. Max, Jeannie, Angela, Vannie and I stopped breathing. Leonard chewed.

What was that sound?

Tap, tap, tap went the sound.

Taaap taptaptaptap tap tap it went again! As if someone were tapping "Shave-and-a-haircut, two bits!"

Taaap taptaptaptap tap tap.

It was coming from INSIDE the hill.

We fell on the hillside, pulling away underbrush and

layers of dead grass.

Behind the underbrush was a rock. It was as tall as Vannie and as fat as two Shacklefords.

"Aunt Sadie, are you in there?" Max called softly.

"Taaap taptaptaptap TAP TAP!" came from inside the hill. "They're in there! They're in there!" Angela and Vannie shouted.

Max, Jeannie, Angela, Vannie and I pushed on the rock while Shackleford dug under it, Chesterton beeped, and Leonard chewed.

The rock didn't budge.

We tried again. Shackleford's digging helped. The rock didn't fit as tightly into the ground anymore.

"It's wobbling," Vannie said. "It's wobbling a little."

We tried again.

The rock wobbled more.

But that was it.

It was one heavy rock.

We tried again while Leonard chewed.

We pushed until our legs slid out from under us and we all collapsed on the ground.

We lay there for a minute to rest, staring into the fog.

"This isn't working," Max groaned. "Think! There has to be a way!"

We lay on the ground, exhausted. Even Shackleford took a break, stretching out on her stomach with her head between her front paws. Even Chesterton shut off his lights and beeper.

I lay flat on my stomach and tried to think, which wasn't easy with Leonard's big, dirty feet in my face.

The idea landed in everybody's brain at once.

"LEONARD!" everybody shouted.

"BELTS!" Max yelled. "Quick, give me all your belts! Jeannie and Angela, go get some of that grass Leonard loves to munch. Joshua, untie Leonard's rope! Shackleford, keep digging!"

We whipped our belts from our jeans and tossed them to Max while Shackleford dug and Chesterton beeped, "beep beepbeepbeepbeep BEEP BEEP!" to keep Supergranny's spirits up.

Max linked the belts into a makeshift harness and hooked it over Leonard's shoulder and around his middle. Then he looped Leonard's rope around the rock and tied both ends to the harness.

By then, Angela and Jeannie were back with armfuls of long grass.

Angela stood at Leonard's north end, urging him to walk toward her for a bite of grass.

"Yum, yum, yummmy grass," she cooed. "Leonard looooves yummmy grass."

Max, Jeannie, Vannie and I stood at Leonard's south end, ready to roll rock.

Leonard took a step, we pushed, the rock wiggled.

Leonard stopped.

"Yuuummm, yummmy grass," Angela cooed, pretending to chew a mouthful of grass herself. Leonard took another step. We pushed. The rock tilted sideways.

Leonard stopped.

"Good Leonard, Leonard looooves yummm yum grass," Angela cooed.

Leonard lunged for the grass. We pushed. The ROCK ROLLED ... revealing an opening into the

36

hillside.

"It's a mine," Max whispered. "An abandoned coal mine entrance!"

Max quickly undid the harness while Angela tossed Leonard the whole tasty armful of grass.

By then, Shackleford and Chesterton were already inside the mine. The rest of us crawled after them, with Max in the lead.

Leonard stayed outside, enjoying supper.

Our flashlights danced around the passageway's walls of black stone. It was cold and dry. After about ten feet, it opened into a small room.

We stopped and beamed our lights around it. Two figures sat on the ground against a wall. It looked as though they were tied hand and foot and had handkerchiefs over their mouths, but it was hard to tell because Shackleford was climbing all over them, licking their faces while Chesterton beeped and whistled in delight.

"Well, hello," Supergranny said as Shackleford grabbed the handkerchief in her teeth and pulled it down around Supergranny's neck. "How was the show?"

"Sorry we missed your act, Jeannie," Dr. Dreamwhopper said. "We were tied up."

8

They'd been surprised in the kitchen. Supergranny had just finished tossing the salad and Dreamwhopper was dumping the spaghetti into the colander to drain when the guys jumped them from behind.

"It's my fault," Dreamwhopper said. "I left the door unlocked when I let Leonard, Shackleford and Chesterton out in the yard to play."

"Nonsense," Supergranny said. "If it's anybody's fault, it's mine. Nobody has sneaked up on me like that in forty years. I must be slipping."

There were four hoodlums, all wearing Halloween moose masks. They took Leonard, Shackleford and Chesterton first, locking them in the barn. Then they left their shoes on the porch, sneaked inside the house in their socks, and surprised Supergranny and

Dreamwhopper.   Afterwards they marched Supergranny and Dreamwhopper out to the mine, questioned them, tied them up and left.

For some reason, they moved Leonard, Shackleford and Chesterton back to the house after that.

At first I couldn't picture how the hoodlums had gotten the drop on Supergranny in the kitchen.

You'd think locking a llama, an Old English sheepdog and a hot-tempered mini-robot in a barn against their will would have been hubbub enough to alert her.

But, no, it wasn't.

"Maybe it was because we were so busy talking about India," Supergranny said.

"We have mutual friends in Delhi," Dreamwhopper explained.

"And Wagner's 'Ride of the Valkyries' was playing on National Public Radio," Supergranny said.

"And we'd turned it up, because it's one of our favorites," Dreamwhopper explained.

The picture got clearer. They'd been partying!

Nobody TURNS UP "Ride of the Valkyries." It's loud even when it's turned down! And, for sure, nobody TRIES TO TALK during "Ride of the Valkyries."

It must have been a madhouse in that kitchen. Spaghetti steaming; Supergranny and Dreamwhopper shouting at each other about Delhi, India; "Ride of the Valkyries" storming out of the radio.

My head hurt just thinking about it. I don't know why the hoodlums didn't roar into the kitchen on motorcycles. Supergranny and Dreamwhopper were having too much fun to notice!

"Well, hey," Max said, his voice cracking slightly, "you're only human."

"Sure," Angela, added. "It could happen to anybody."

"No, it was my fault," Dreamwhopper insisted, shaking his silver hair out of his eyes. "I'd been warned. I should have told Sadie about this mystery business at once. I wanted to get acquainted first, then tell her at dinner. I should never have waited."

Supergranny patted his arm. "Tell me now, Delano," she said. "Tell us all."

*   *   *   *

We sat in a circle, our flashlights casting strange shadows as the walls murmured echoes of Dreamwhopper's story.

It began in 1799 when a son was born into a rich English shipbuilding family. The boy, Calvin Kepplewait, was a sturdy and charming child — maybe *too* charming. He was spoiled by his parents and grew to be greedy and self-centered.

He hated schooling but loved the sea. At sixteen he talked his parents into letting him sail for the Orient on a family merchant ship.

For four years he crisscrossed the seven seas. By age twenty he was first mate on the *Forever Gold* a type of cargo sailing ship called "East Indiamen" that was armed with guns to fight off pirates. He was a good sailor and still oozed charm — but had a reputation for being greedy and self-centered underneath.

On April 13, 1819, the ship docked in Bombay, India, for a seven-week layover to be repaired and loaded with silks and spices.

The morning after docking, Calvin left with an Indian guide to visit Bombay's Elephanta Caves carvings.

He never returned.

The captain wasn't worried at first. Calvin often took off for days on mysterious errands when the ship docked at exotic ports.

There wasn't much the captain could do about it. After all, Calvin *was* the boss' son.

Seven weeks passed. The *Forever Gold* was shipshape again, the hold was stuffed with spices and silk, and the crew was homesick for wives, girlfriends and children. Everybody was eager to sail for England.

But where was Calvin?

There was a rumor he'd fallen in love with a maharajah's daughter in Delhi. The captain sent a search party.

No Calvin.

There was a rumor he'd joined a notorious gang of temple thieves in their Himalayan mountain hideout. The captain sent a search party.

No Calvin.

After three months, the *Forever Gold* sailed without him. The captain knew he'd be in deep trouble for leaving the boss' son behind — but what could he do?

Calvin had vanished. His family never saw him again.

Thirteen years passed ... then, in 1832, *a rich, mysterious stranger appeared in the southeastern Ohio hills.*

"The stranger wore white silk suits and lizard boots and called himself Caleb Keptheart," Dreamwhopper said.

"And he spoke with an English accent and rode a palomino called 'Forever Gold,'" Angela added.

"Right," Dreamwhopper said, then filled in Supergranny on all that Jeannie had told us driving to the farm: about the rumors that Keptheart's fortune had come from a card game or from robbing a diamond mine. About how Keptheart had founded OKU, built the town, designed the courthouse, served in the Ohio legislature, married a descendant of Daniel Boone and taken Charles Dickens and Mark Twain to lunch — at different times, of course. About how he'd owned 3,000 acres when he died.

"And this farm was his last holding," Dreamwhopper said. "Caleb's only son lived here until he died in 1927."

"But why do you think Caleb Keptheart is Calvin Kepplewait?" Angela asked. "And even if he was, what's the big mystery NOW??"

Dreamwhopper stared at her, but didn't seem to see her. He focused on the past, more than 150 years ago, on a mysterious stranger astride a golden horse.

When he spoke again, it was in a whisper.

We gathered closer.

"Five years ago when I moved into the farmhouse, I started what I thought would be a simple remodeling job — new bookcases in the living room. But I forgot the Remodeler's Cardinal Rule.

"There Is No Simple Remodeling Job," Supergranny put in.

"That's it." Dreamwhopper nodded. "Remodeling Rule 1. The living room was wallpapered in eagles as big as dinner plates. Mildewed eagles. You know mildew, those brown fungus spots that sometimes attack things like wallpaper when they get wet and don't dry fast enough."

"Of course, it can smell bad and spread," Angela put in. "I once did a report on mildew and —"

"Not now, dear," Supergranny said, mercifully saving us from spending the whole night in an abandoned coal mine hearing a mildew report.

"Smell is right, Angela. I was afraid if I built the bookcase OVER the wallpaper, the smell would stay and the mildew might even spread to my books. So I steamed off the eagles.

"Underneath the eagles was wallpaper of people

43

dressed to the nines and dancing under trellises or grape arbors or something of the sort, so I steamed them off, too.

"Underneath the dancing trellises were roses big as pumpkins and I considered forgetting the whole thing and leaving my books in crates, but the roses made me dizzy and Leonard bilious so I steamed them off, too, and finally got down to the bare plaster.

"All those layers of wallpaper had disguised just how awful the plaster was. Where it didn't wave, it bulged, and where it didn't wave or bulge, it had cracks or holes, so I had to rip out the old wall down to the studs and that's where I found it, tucked between a stud and the back of the fireplace."

He stopped and gazed into space again. Back 150-plus years again, I guess.

"Found what, Delano?" Supergranny prodded.

"A small, locked tin box. The box, don't you see, gave me the connection between Caleb Keptheart and Calvin Kepplewait and the source of their — I mean his — mysterious fortune.

"After I found it, I was determined to write a biography of Keptheart and solve the mystery of his past. I've been researching for five years. For the past two, Max has helped, feeding the research into the computer."

"And what was in the box?" Vannie asked.

"Three things," the professor answered slowly.

"One: Faded letters in brown ink addressed to Calvin P. Kepplewait, dated 1819."

"Whoa," Angela said.

"Two: An article from the old Strand magazine

about the famous Orloff diamond, given to Russian Empress Catherine II by her lover Prince Gregory Orloff. The article said the diamond was rumored to have been plucked from the eye of an idol during a rash of robberies of Indian temples. Most of the other jewels were believed to have been hidden somewhere in India. They were never recovered."

"Fascinating," Supergranny said.

"I thought so," Dreamwhopper agreed. "My theory is that Keptheart got his hands on that stash of stolen diamonds and founded his fortune with part of them."

"And the rest?" Angela asked.

"Hid them," Dreamwhopper said.

"Hold on," I said. "I think I know what the third thing in that box was."

"DIAMONDS!!" Vannie yelled. "Big ones!" That's what the thieves were after today! DIAMONDS!!"

Dreamwhopper shook his head.

"Nope. They were after the map. That was the third thing in the box: the map. The map that can lead us to *one hundred million dollars' worth of diamonds.*"

10

It was a good yarn, but I was too nervous to enjoy it.

I kept imagining the flickering shadows were returning moose.

Frankly, sitting in a spooky mine shaft on a foggy night with four thugs in moose masks likely to return any minute made me feel insecure.

We hadn't even posted a guard, unless you counted Leonard out there chewing his cud. Who knew what kind of a watch llama Leonard was? He impressed me as leading a sheltered life. Would he neigh or whinny or screech if the thugs showed up or just nod gently and stick to chewing cud?

And if he did warn us, what then? A pell-mell race deeper into a dark, abandoned mine no doubt full of dropoffs, collapsed tunnels, murky, wet filth, hungry bats and assorted rodents?

THAT would be jolly.

I'd have felt a lot more secure back at the farmhouse with the doors locked and the lights on.

True, from untying Supergranny and Dreamwhopper to hearing his whole story, even counting all his gazing into time and space, probably only ten minutes clock time had passed.

But it had taken several hours' toll of my nerves, and I was definitely ready to break camp.

Unfortunately, the rest of them were chattering happily as picnickers at the beach. They were chattering about maps.

Somehow, the thugs had found out about Dreamwhopper's secret map (I was pretty sure I knew how). Already they'd busted into the farmhouse twice this month while he was away. (Doesn't say much for Leonard's watchllama skills, does it?)

But they hadn't found the map.

This time, they'd evidently figured they had to catch Dreamwhopper himself and make him cough it up.

He'd refused at first. That had thrown their leader, whom the others had called "Main Moose," into a tizzy fit, and he'd searched the house.

No map.

"They all regrouped in the kitchen, madder than trapped skunks," Dreamwhopper said. "At that point it seemed prudent to give them the map."

"Oh no," Angela groaned. "You mean those phony moose have the wonderful diamonds?"

Dreamwhopper laughed. "No, sirree! Angela. *Those phony moose have a phony map!*

"The real map is hidden safely back on campus. As soon as Max and I suspected somebody knew about our research, we drew up a phony one. We spilled tea on it and let Leonard nibble its edges to make it look old."

"It led them to another map in a hollow, buckeye tree down by the Hocking River," Max said, chuckling.

"Which led them to another map in a dumpster behind K-Mart in Lancaster, Ohio," Dreamwhopper added.

"Which led them to the police station in downtown Keptheart," Max finished with a grin.

"Which means they're going to realize they've been had and come running back here in about—" Dreamwhopper studied his watch " —an hour!"

"Oh dear," Supergranny said. "You think the time is that short? Then I suppose we should get cracking."

She whipped a notepad and ballpoint out of her pocket. Finally, action. I felt more secure already.

"I suggest we define our goals, make our plans and divide into teams," she said.

Everybody agreed.

"That should take about—" she glanced at her watch again "—Two minutes."

Dreamwhopper, Max and Jeannie laughed. They thought she was kidding. They didn't know her as well as the rest of us did.

"Angela, Goal 1?"

"Find the diamonds?" Angela asked.

Supergranny smiled. "That's important, but let's put that as Goal 2. Remember, safety before diamonds. Joshua, Goal 1?"

"Catch the Moose Gang?" I asked.

"Bingo," Supergranny said. "To review: Goal 1, catch the Moose Gang. Goal 2, find the diamonds."

"Let's use Plan 231XYZ."

Plan 231XYZ went like this:

Team A, Jeannie and Vannie, would drive to town for the sheriff, then return to the mine.

Team B, Supergranny and Professor Dreamwhopper, had the hardest job: bait. They had to sit in the mine as though they were still tied up while we rolled the rock back over the mine opening. The idea was that they'd act like nothing had happened since the moose left. When the moose came storming back into the mine after the REAL map, the sheriff would jump them. We hoped.

Team C, Max, Angela and I, had several unpleasant little chores that I'll get to in a minute.

After we bagged the moose, we'd regroup to retrieve the real map, crack the code and find the diamonds. Nothing could be simpler, except maybe advanced calculus or writing Latin poetry.

By now I was ninety-percent sure Hooded Sweatshirt had been stealing information about the maps and diamonds from Max's computer. So I laid that little bombshell on them before we scattered. Everybody agreed Hooded Sweatshirt must be the leak, but nobody had time to worry about who he was.

We were too busy getting ready for a pack of moose.

Team A took off for town, and Team C (Max, Angela, and I) left Team B in the mine and headed back through the fog to the farmhouse, dragging

Leonard, Shackleford and Chesterton behind.

The last three were not happy campers. To lure the moose into ambush, we had to convince them nothing had changed since they'd left. That meant L.S.C., as Angela called Leonard, Shackleford and Chesterton for short, had to be re-locked in the farmhouse.

Supergranny had PERSONALLY explained this to them before we left the mine. She'd stressed their importance in the whole operation. She'd promised them their favorite treats (grass, Milk Bones and gumdrops). She'd petted, praised, coaxed and bribed.

But the minute they were out of her sight, they began to balk, sulk, quarrel and fuss until I would gladly have traded them for a handful of beans, like Jack traded his cow.

They wouldn't even have to be cash beans. A check would do.

Finally, no thanks to L.S.C., we made it to the farmhouse.

And what did they do when they got there?

After all the pouting, fuss and ruckus?

THEY REMEMBERED THEY WERE TIRED. THEY DECIDED THEY WERE GLAD TO BE HOME. THEY SETTLED DOWN FOR A NICE NAP!

11

We were ready for them ... sort of.

Team A (Jeannie and Vannie) had taken the Ferrari to town for the sheriff and, I hoped, were back hiding around the mine with about a hundred sheriff's deputies.

Team B (Supergranny and Dreamwhopper) were in the mine pretending to be tied up. Max, Angela and I had rolled the rock back in front of the entrance. It was much easier rolling it back down into its hole than it had been rolling it out — or would have been if Max hadn't stopped every two inches to apologize and ask, "Are you SURE about this, Aunt Sadie?"

"Absolutely. Keep rolling, Max," Supergranny reassured him about forty-eight times.

"Has to be done, Max," Dreamwhopper put in.

"Only way to fool those moose."

They grinned and coaxed and grinned and coaxed until the danged boulder thudded into place, missing my foot by a millimeter.

Next, Max had to hide Team C in a secret closet back at the farmhouse. The hiding place had been built right into the staircase wall when old Caleb built the house. You stepped into it through a trapdoor under a braided rug in the small bedroom upstairs.

Max must have used up all his apologizing on Supergranny and Dreamwhopper, because slamming the trapdoor shut on Team C didn't seem to bother him a bit.

Angela and I were Team C. Lucky us.

The closet, really a small box just below the second floor, was too small to stand up in, and we sat back to back with Angela peering through a peephole into the kitchen and me peering through a peephole into the living room. I couldn't see much, but at least I could hear old L.S.C. snoring.

Max whispered goodbye and slipped outside. He was to hide near the mine and help those hundreds of sheriff's deputies I hoped were there.

Our job had three parts:

1. Hide until the moose came back and pick up any information we could through the peepholes.

2. After the moose left, stay put for a count of 300 (to keep from getting overeager and running right into them.)

3. Spring Leonard, Shackleford and Chesterton, then follow the moose to the mine at a safe distance to also help those hundreds of sheriff's deputies.

I've tried out a variety of hiding places since we met Supergranny and this one wasn't bad.

It beat hanging onto a vine on a window ledge like in our first case with Supergranny, *The Mystery of the Shrunken Heads*. And, mercifully, there weren't any snakes like when I hid out on Magic Island in *The Case of the Riverboat Riverbelle*.

So it wasn't bad.

But I was tired and it was boring, and I just wished the moose would show up and get it over with. It *was* past 1 a.m. and we *had* driven 520 miles to get here.

After being cooped up about 20 minutes, I began to notice how hard the floor was.

Worse, "Miss Elbows," otherwise known as Angela, was hogging all the space.

"Cripes, Angela, could you kindly get your elbow out of my kidney?" I whispered.

"Quiet," she hissed.

"For Pete's sake, just turn a little sideways to get your el—"

At that, she jabbed me so hard it knocked the wind out of me. Before I could catch my breath she grabbed my hair, whipped my head around 140 degrees and pointed my nose at the kitchen peephole.

There was a light. Someone was moving around downstairs.

*   *   *   *

The moose were back, and they suspected something.

One of them was standing with the back of his head about a foot from the peephole. He was so close all

53

we could see were his antlers, but we could hear him fine.

"What was that? I heard something," he was whispering to his fellow moose.

"Quiet," his fellow moose whispered gruffly. "Don't wake the infernal livestock; I don't want to deal with any more llama spit."

"Well, I HEARD something," Moose 1 insisted in a whiny voice.

Rats. The truth was, they'd heard me. I'd wrecked the whole operation. That'll teach me to fight with my sisters. How many times has Mom told us not to fight? Ten million? Twenty?

If we could just get out of this one, I'd never fight with Angela again. Never. I don't care how many times she jabbed me with her elbows — just so that moose didn't find the trapdoor.

The antlers moved out of view; we could hear the moose sneaking around the house.

If we could get out of this one, I wouldn't even fight with Vannie.

Someone crept up the stairs.

Someone crossed the room above our head.

Someone stood on our trapdoor.

Someone barked!

"**#xx! It's just the dog," a gruff moose said.

"Spooked by a hairy dog," a female moose said with an ugly laugh.

Shackleford had covered for me! They thought she'd made all the noise!

"So, I made a mistake," Whiny Moose answered. "Let's get out of here before the llama wakes up. I've had it with llama spit, too."

Hooray for Leonard! He must have spit on them good before! I took back my doubts about his watchllama skills!

We heard them creeping back downstairs, trying not to wake Leonard, but they were too late.

Leonard was up, ready to spit and chase moose.

The battle was on, and I'd never seen or heard anything like it. Angela and I kept trading peepholes so we could watch the whole thing.

Moose were jumping over chairs and knocking over furniture with Leonard, Shackleford and Chesterton hot on their heels.

Every time a moose would get to the door to make a run for it, Leonard or Shackleford or Chesterton would be there first, snarling and barking and spitting and whirring.

I hadn't seen Chesterton and Shackleford have so much fun since they'd chased the princess at Heidelberg Castle.

And I didn't even know Leonard HAD fun.

Finally Female Moose got the kitchen door open and held off the livestock with a kitchen chair while Gruff Moose and Whiny Moose escaped.

She threw the chair at Shackleford who dodged just in time, flipped the lock on the inside and slammed the door behind her.

Angela and I counted to 300 in whispers while I tried not to think of one burning question.

Why were there only three moose?

12

"Two hundred and ninety-eight, two hundred and ninety-nine, THREE HUNDRED!"

We pushed open the trapdoor, climbed into the bedroom and raced downstairs. Leonard, Shackleford and Chesterton were still jumping and lunging and spitting at the back door, eager for "Moose Chase -- Part II."

Poor Professor Dreamwhopper's *formerly* tidy farmhouse looked like the scene of a buffalo stampede in a tornado.

The overturned tables, chairs and lamps and the books knocked from their shelves weren't so bad. Neither were the broken dishes and torn curtains.

But the spaghetti sauce that had been bumped off the stove, splattered on the walls and floors, and tracked through the house in greasy, orange globs ... Ugh! A disaster!

As much as we'd have *liked* to clean up the mess, we really didn't have time. After all, our orders had been to follow the moose at a safe distance.

"Remember, SAFE DISTANCE," I kept reminding L.S.C. as I snapped on Shackleford's leash.

"That's right, SAFE DISTANCE," Angela echoed as she grabbed Leonard and unlocked the back door.

Of course, "safe distance" didn't mean squat to them. They hit the back door like a racetrack starting gate.

Whoosh! We were off.

        *   *   *   *

Meanwhile, down at the mine there was trouble, although we didn't know it at the time. Here's what happened, according to Max's eyewitness account:

He'd been lying in the bushes directly opposite the mine entrance wondering where the heck the cavalry was. You'll remember that Jeannie and Vannie had roared off in the Ferrari for help. They should have been back by now with the sheriff and deputies.

Well, they weren't.

For all Max knew, the Ferrari had stalled, or run into a ditch in the fog, or — chilling thought — been stopped by four guys in moose masks.

Just as he heard the racket the moose made getting themselves out of the farmhouse and to the trail, he FINALLY heard Jeannie and Vannie thrashing up the hill behind him with help.

That was the good news.

The bad news was the sheriff's department was so busy dealing with homecoming weekend, patrolling county roads and all, that they could spare just one deputy.

"His name's 'Cool,'" Jeannie whispered as she slid into place beside Max. "Deputy Cool."

Deputy Cool sat down under a willow tree and gave Max a mock salute.

"I don't think he's taking this seriously," Jeannie whispered.

"He thinks we're all kooks," Vannie whispered. "He's never heard of a Supergranny, world-famous detective, but he *has* heard Dreamwhopper lives with a llama. He doesn't believe the story of the guys in the moose masks, and he thinks we're all weird. Batty. Kooks."

Max, Jeannie and Vannie lay on their stomachs in the bushes, their eyes peeled on the boulder blocking the mine entrance. Deputy Cool leaned back against the tree trunk, twiddled his thumbs and yawned.

After the ruckus the moose had made leaving the farmhouse, they hadn't made a sound.

The night was still.

Suddenly, a shadow appeared to the right of the boulder.

A shadow with antlers.

Deputy Cool stopped twiddling his thumbs.

Another figure with antlers appeared out of the fog.

They started rocking the boulder to-and-fro, to-and-fro.

A third antlered figure joined them.

To-and-fro, to-and-fro.

Vannie held up three fingers at Max and frowned. Where was Moose Four?

Max shrugged as if to say, "I don't know."

Where *was* Moose Four?? Sneaking up behind them? Still back at the farmhouse? Had he found Angela and Joshua?

Nobody knew.

At last the boulder rolled away from the mine.

"NOW!" Max yelled. He, Jeannie and Deputy Cool leaped for the moose from the outside as planned. Supergranny and Dreamwhopper leaped for the moose from inside as planned.

They all collided at the line of scrimmage.

"Got 'im!" Max yelled. "Got 'im!" Jeannie yelled. "Got 'im!" Cool yelled. "That's me!" Dreamwhopper yelled.

The upshot was, Max and Supergranny had bagged one moose fore and aft, Jeannie and Dreamwhopper had bagged another fore and aft, and Deputy Cool had bagged Dreamwhopper.

That meant they were short one moose.

"HE'S GETTING AWAY!" screamed Vannie, who had stayed in the bushes as lookout. "HE'S RUNNING BACK UP THE TRAIL!"

And so he was, racing back up the foggy trail toward the farmhouse, just as Leonard, Shackleford, Chesterton, Angela and I were *quietly* racing down the trail to the mine.

It was a horrendous crash.

I don't know who was the most shocked. One second a moosehead BURSTS out of the fog, and the next we're all in a pile, skidding down the hillside, bumping into trees and rocks, screaming, yelling, screeching, barking, whirring and blinking.

It was a shock and a nightmare and I'd just as soon never do it again.

Picture yourself careening down a steep hillside in thick fog tangled up with a llama, sheepdog, robot and criminal moose, and you'll see what I mean.

While you're at it, picture Vannie at the top of the trail, shouting instructions.

"GRAB THE MOOSE! DON'T LET HIM GET AWAY! GRAB HIM!" she shouted.

Instructions were the last thing we needed. What we needed was to STOP rolling down the hill. What we needed was to NOT fall off a cliff, land in the road and get run over. What we needed was to NOT be trampled by a llama or gored by fake moose antlers.

What we DID NOT NEED were instructions.

Luckily, good ol' Leonard kept his footing, managing not to squash any of us, including the moose, and our whole tangled mess finally slid to a stop against a poison sumac.

"I GIVE UP! CALL OFF THE LLAMA! CALL OFF THE LLAMA!" the moose screamed.

We marched him back up to the trail where everybody else was waiting. Then we marched all three moose back to the farmhouse for a council meeting.

Dreamwhopper was somewhat dismayed at the state of his farmhouse with its dried spaghetti globs, but he was a sport about it.

"We can't worry about a little spaghetti sauce now," he said. "There's still a loose moose. We've got to find those diamonds before he does."

"You're so right, Delano," Supergranny agreed. "On to Plan B!"

13

Where was Moose Four?

Nobody knew, except maybe the three Mooseketeers we'd bagged, and they weren't talking. In the living room, Deputy Cool read them their right to remain silent while we had our council meeting in the kitchen. Then he asked them about Moose Four, but they wouldn't talk.

"I want to call my lawyer," said Female Moose.

"Me, too," said Whiny Moose.

"Ditto," said Gruff Moose.

After our council meeting, we helped get the moose into Deputy Cool's squad car and then formed a caravan to the county jail.

Max and Jeannie rode with Deputy Cool to help keep an eye on the moose; Supergranny followed in her Ferrari with Vannie, Angela, Shackleford and Chesterton; and Dreamwhopper and I brought up the rear in his Jeep.

I felt bad about leaving Leonard behind, but Dreamwhopper insisted he liked staying home and would relish the peace and quiet.

All of us except the moose let Leonard kiss our cheeks to say goodbye. Deputy Cool almost chickened out, but didn't.

"Yech," whined Whiny Moose.

We ignored him.

By 3 a.m., all three moose and Deputy Cool were tucked into the county jail. The rest of us were hovering around Max's computer, whispering so we wouldn't wake the whole dorm.

Max wanted to be sure Hooded Sweatshirt hadn't messed up his files.

He hadn't. Everything looked OK.

"While you're at it, you'd better change the name of the file to make it harder for the next snooper," Jeannie advised. "'CalebK' is a dead giveaway."

Max had filed everything about Caleb Keptheart and the diamonds under "CalebK," making it pretty easy for anyone who broke into his computer to find the information.

That may sound dumb, but who would suspect someone would break into your computer after a research project you were working on for a professor? Not me.

"Meanwhile, lock your door when you're not in the room," Supergranny advised.

"And call security to change the lock," Dreamwhopper advised.

"OK. Roger. Right," Max answered absently, his mind on a new password. It had to be eight letters or less.

"How about Dnomaid?" he asked.

"You mean 'DIAMOND' spelled backward? Too easy," Angela said.

"How about ForeverG?" Vannie asked. "After Caleb's horse, 'Forever Gold.'"

"That's a sure tip-off to anybody who knows anything about Caleb," Dreamwhopper said.

"Besides, it looks too interesting," Angela added. "If Hooded Sweatshirt couldn't find a file about Caleb, he'd probably check all the interesting-sounding files next. You need a boring file name."

"You're right," Max said. "What's a boring word with eight letters or less?"

"Homework?" I suggested.

"Dryclean." "Gutters." "Kale." "Ironing." "Eggplant." "Chores." "Meeting." "Dental," the others whispered.

"I'll take 'dryclean' for now," Max said. "And change it to 'chores' next week."

That settled, we had to get the map.

You'll remember Dreamwhopper said it was hidden "safely back on campus."

You'll never guess where.

In a safety deposit box at the bank? Between the mattress and springs? In the toe of a boot in the closet? In a book?

Naaah.

Dreamwhopper and Max were too clever for that.

They'd hidden it right smack dab in the middle of campus.

And nothing would do but for us to race across campus to get it. Right now. At 3:30 a.m. This minute.

After all, this was the moment Dreamwhopper had been waiting for since he'd heard Supergranny would visit OKU.

"That map is a mystery itself," he explained. "A code of some kind. Max and I can't make head nor tail of it. But, Sadie, with your detective experience, it should be a cinch," he told Supergranny.

"I had planned to explain the whole story over dinner, then you and I could retrieve the map in time to meet the kids at the Comedy Show," he whispered as we walked through the night across the deserted campus.

Of course, his plan had gone awry when the moose showed up.

And it was about to go awry again.

Remember the statue of Caleb Keptheart on horseback?

The one just inside the campus gate?

The one thousands and thousands and thousands of students walked past every day?

Remember how Caleb was holding his hat?

Well, between his granite hand and his granite hat there was a small hole — just big enough for a treasure map.

And that's where the map was.

The problem was ... *Caleb was gone!*

That's right, old Granite Caleb was gone, horse and

all. Nothing was left but his granite pedestal.

Dreamwhopper was speechless. *Everybody* was speechless.

We stood there in the dark, blinking our eyes and rubbing the palms of our hands across the pedestal like maybe the statue had turned invisible and we'd be able to FEEL it even if we couldn't SEE it.

"I can't understand it," Dreamwhopper finally managed to gasp. "He's been sitting there for sixty years. He weighs half a ton. Where did he *go*?"

"Check the bushes," Supergranny suggested.

We fanned out and checked behind and under every bush on the main campus green.

No Caleb. No horse.

Of course, right away we suspected the loose moose. But how could he have found out about the map? And how could one moose have moved a 1,000-pound statue? And why? Why not just take the map??

"Supergranny," Vannie said, "There's —"

"Not now, dear," Supergranny interrupted. "Max, could Hooded Sweatshirt have discovered the map's whereabouts from your computer?"

"Impossible, Aunt Sadie," Max answered. "I didn't write the map's location *anywhere*."

"But, Supergranny," Angela said, "it —"

"Not now, dear," Supergranny interrupted. "Delano, are you absolutely sure nobody saw you hide it?"

"Absolutely," Dreamwhopper and Max said.

"Supergranny," Angela and Vannie said together, "We —"

66

"Just a minute, girls. And, neither of you told anybody about the hiding place?" Supergranny asked.

"Not a soul," Max and Dreamwhopper said together.

"IT WASN'T MOOSE!" Angela and Vannie yelled.

"At least, it wasn't our loose moose," Angela went on. "It was a homecoming game prank by Mudville students. Look! A note!"

A piece of lined yellow legal paper was taped down at the base of the statue's pedestal.

Supergranny whipped a flashlight out of her purse, and we all crowded around to see:

Old Caleb Rode His Horse
To Join The Victors — Us, Of Course.
You Won't Get Him Home Again
Unless Tomorrow's Game You Win.
  —The Mudville Moose

"Oh, no," Max groaned. "Some Mudville students have swiped Caleb as a homecoming prank. Last year some OKU students swiped the Mudville Victory Bell. They pulled it around the stadium in a wagon during the game and rang it every time we scored."

Professor Dreamwhopper smacked his forehead with his hand. "A PRANK! SOME MUDVILLE STUDENTS HAVE SWIPED THE STATUE AS A PRANK! OF ALL THE JUVENILE, IRRESPONSIBLE, LOW-DOWN, CHILDISH —"

He went on that way for some time. I couldn't blame him, but I wished he hadn't.

If the Mudville students had just swiped Caleb as a

prank, the statue would probably be at tomorrow's game. Maybe we could get the map then, with nobody the wiser.

All was not lost.

Or wouldn't have been if we hadn't made so much hullabaloo right there at the statue, tipping off anyone who happened to be watching that the map was hidden in the statue.

And although we didn't know it at the time ... someone was watching.

Oh, yes ... *someone was watching.*

14

It was one of those perfect homecoming game afternoons when the air is sharp and sun-splashed and the world wears its brightest colors.

People streamed toward the stadium, laughing and joking and holding tightly to children's hands as they crossed long, slow-moving rivers of traffic. Band members in dark green uniforms with white satin capes gathered on street corners to play trumpets, tubas and trombones, while somewhere a bass drum called to your heart, "Beat faster, beat faster, keep time."

I was disguised as a kangaroo.

So was Max. Well, he wasn't disguised, exactly. He was the Ohio Keptheart Kangaroos' official mascot kangaroo who helped lead cheers at the football games.

I was his deputy kangaroo or apprentice or assistant or whatever, and it wasn't easy. I had to carry my tail in my hand to keep from tripping on it and had to hold my neck stiff so my eyes would line up right with the eye holes in the kangaroo's neck.

"I itch. I think my suit has fleas. Does yours itch, Joshua?" asked Vannie, also a deputy kangaroo.

"Not until you brought it up," I said. Drat, why did she have to mention fleas? Just thinking about fleas lurking in my kangaroo fur made me itch.

"It's your imagination," Max said as we joined Jeannie, who was a cheerleader, on the grass in front of the OKU student section. "Try to stop scratching; jump up and down and wave to the fans."

The stands were filling up and we were supposed to help the cheerleaders whip the fans into a frenzy before the game started.

That was our *official* job.

Our *unofficial* job was to find the Caleb statue and secure the treasure map.

That's how Dreamwhopper put it: "Secure the treasure map."

He, Supergranny and Angela, along with Shackleford and Chesterton, were subbing for Max, selling burritos at the Burrito Buggy on the main campus. They would close five minutes before kickoff and join us at the stadium.

We tried to keep one eye on the Mudville side of the field for a glimpse of Caleb's statue while we led cheers and did tricks with the cheerleaders.

Pretty soon, I forgot the minuses and began to see

the pluses of wearing a kangaroo suit.

For one thing, if you goof, nobody knows it's you.

For another, people cheer almost anything you do. Wave — they cheer. Jump — they cheer. Twirl your tail — they cheer.

Max and the cheerleaders knelt in a leapfrog line and Vannie and I jumped over them.

Five thousand people cheered!

We did a cancan while the pep band played the Ohio Keptheart Fight Song.

Ten thousand people cheered!

We turned somersaults clear across the field to the Mudville side.

Fifteen thousand people cheered!

I got so caught up in the glory, I turned around and started somersaulting back. Max grabbed me midfield.

"Hang on, Josh, we're supposed to shake hands with the Mudville cheerleaders and mascots while we're over here."

"And look for the statue, dumbacre," Vannieroo hissed.

My kangaroo head was whopperjawed from the somersaulting, and I couldn't see out. I tried to adjust my eyeholes while Max and Vannie dragged me back to the Mudville side.

Just as I reached out to shake hands with a Mudville mascot, I finally lined one eye up with a hole.

"Aggggh!" I yelled.

Antlers!

*   *   *   *

I shouldn't have been so shocked. I knew in theory

71

that the Mudville team was nicknamed the "Mudville Moose" just as the Ohio Keptheart team was nicknamed the "Keptheart Kangaroos."

Everybody is nicknamed something: Iowa University Hawkeyes, Ohio University Bobcats, Notre Dame Fighting Irish, West Virginia Mountaineers, Ohio State Buckeyes, *something*.

But I hadn't planned on reeling out of a dozen somersaults smack into a pair of antlers after all we'd been through last night with those outlaw moose.

I was still shaking when we got back to the OKU side for the kickoff. Max sat me down on the bench with the team to chill out.

Vannie was prancing around with Max and some of the cheerleaders, but Jeannie came over to buck me up.

"I'm sorry," I apologized. "I didn't mean to be rude. I know *all* people dressed up as moose aren't bad. I think it was a delayed reaction to rolling down the hill in the fog with the moose last night. And I think I need more sleep. I'm not used to going to bed at 4 a.m."

"Don't worry about it," Jeannie said, patting my paw. "Besides, there *is* something fishy over there — GO, BEN!!" she screamed loud as a fire drill. We jumped to our feet. You remember Ben, No. 33, the running back, Max's best friend? He had caught a lateral pass, he was crossing Mudville's 35-yard line, he was on the 30, he was on the 20, he was ... down. But what a run!

Good ol' Ben. How could I have suspected him of being sneaky Hooded Sweatshirt?

"What's fishy?" I whispered to Jeannie as OKU huddled.

"Too many moose!" Jeannie yelled, clapping her hands and kicking to the fight song.

The quarterback snapped the ball, a long pass to — no, wait — it was a fake. The quarterback was handing it off to Ben. Ben was crossing the ten. He was crossing the goal. Touchdown!

The fans cheered, the band played, and we kangaroos jumped up and down and hugged the cheerleaders, then hugged some more as Keptheart's kick sailed through the goal post, scoring the extra point.

"There are supposed to be six moose," Jeannie whispered as I hugged her. "But there are seven."

I stared across the field at the Mudville Moose mascots. They were moving around so much, they were hard to count. Finally they lined up to do their famous kickoff moo.

Jeannie was wrong. There weren't seven. There were ten.

15

"AHHHHHHHHHHHHHHHH," the Mudville Moose chanted as the OKU kicker raced toward the ball.

"AHHHHHHHHHHHH ... MOO!" they yelled as he kicked it.

Uh-oh. It wasn't such a hot kick. It took a weird bounce on the forty and popped into the loving arms of Mudville's No. 83. He dodged to the left and lit out down the far side of the field. An OKU tackle was reaching for him, reaching, reach —

SLAM! A Mudville blocker got our tackle.

No. 83 was in the clear, he was on the twenty, the ten, the five. Uh-oh, he scored.

You'd think Mudville had never scored a touchdown before, the way they carried on about one measly little kickoff return. Fans jumping up and down, moose

dancing, moose pulling a wagon 'round the field with a
— WITH THE STOLEN STATUE OF CALEB
KEPTHEART!

I don't know where they'd had the statue stashed,
but they must have been saving it to celebrate their
first touchdown. They were pulling it back and forth in
front of the Mudville cheering section, prancing around
and screaming like hyenas.

"There it is! After it!" Max yelled.

"But, but, but — " I was trying to say, "But the
game is starting."

It was. Mudville's extra-point kicker was in place.

The umpire was blowing his whistle.

The ball was in motion.

None of this fazed Max.

"We've got to get that map before someone else
does!" Max yelled, barreling across the field.

Jeannie and Vannie barreled after him.

I did not want to run onto the playing field with a
game going on. Not in front of thirty thousand
people. Not even in front of thirty people. Not now.
Not ever.

But I didn't want to let Dreamwhopper and Max
down, either. Or let a major diamond treasure fall into
the hands of an outlaw moose. Or let Vannie rush to
the rescue while I sat on the bench.

To heck with it! I grabbed my tail and raced
straight across the 50-yard line.

By now, the two moose pulling the Caleb statue
wagon realized three kangaroos and a cheerleader
were after them.

They thought we were trying to get the statue back.

They were determined to keep it unless OKU won the game. After all, OKU had kept THEIR victory bell the year before until Mudville won the game. By their lights, it was only fair for OKU to win Caleb back on the playing field.

Of course, we weren't after the statue.

We were after the map.

They didn't know that.

The closer we got to the wagon, the faster they ran.

They ran onto the field.

We chased.

They ran toward the OKU goal.

We chased.

Meanwhile, an awkward situation was getting worse. Something had happened at the other end of the field.

OKU had blocked the extra-point kick.

An OKU player had the ball.

He was running our way.

Everybody was running our way.

The announcer was booming, "Please clear the field," the umpires were throwing flags, the stands were going nuts.

The OKU player was running beside me, clutching the ball.

Eleven Mudville players and ten OKU players and I don't know how many moose mascots were gaining on us.

An Old English sheepdog and small robot passed us.

Up ahead, Max jumped onto the Caleb wagon.

A moose jumped onto the wagon with him.

Max was waving something over his head. He had the map!

He tossed it TO ME!

I caught it. Now what?

A moose was running on my left — was he the outlaw moose?

A moose was running on my right — was he the outlaw moose?

They were reaching for me.

"Toss it, Joshua, quick, I'm in the clear," yelled the moose on my right. It was a familiar voice. It was SUPERGRANNY! SOMEHOW, FOR SOME REASON, SUPERGRANNY WAS DRESSED AS A MOOSE!

The moose on my left had me! He was trying to grab the map from my hand. I passed it to Supergranny as I went down.

THUD, I hit the turf. THUD, the moose landed on me. Thudthudthudthud, several more moose mascots and several more moose players, piled on. THUD! Some laggard landed on top.

It was dark and noisy on the bottom of the pile. I couldn't breathe and I probably had 138 broken bones. We'd all probably go to jail for disturbing the peace of a football game. Max might be expelled from OKU and Professor Dreamwhopper fired.

But VICTORY was ours!

WE'D WON! We had the map!

*   *   *   *

The game was delayed while they checked me for broken bones.

And while the umpire and two campus security guards questioned us.

And while another campus security guard called the police and sheriff.

And while the chief of campus security made all ten moose mascots line up and remove their antler masks to be identified.

Six moose were official, card-carrying, Mudville student mascots.

One of them, as you know, was Supergranny.

Another turned out to be Dreamwhopper.

A third was Angela.

(I'll explain later what they were doing in moose suits. The important thing now is to note that nine moose had been identified.)

Moose Ten was the one who had tried to grab the map out of my hands.

NOBODY on either side could identify him — except Dreamwhopper.

"Rex?" he asked. "Aren't you my former student Rex? What are you doing dressed as a moose?"

Rex Moose wasn't talking, except to demand to see his lawyer.

For sure, he was our Fourth Moose.

The sheriff took him off to county jail to call his lawyer. The police let the rest of us off with a warning and we sat down to watch the game.

The umpire refused to count the last play because there had been three kangaroos, ten moose, a stolen statue, an Old English sheepdog, a mini-robot and a cheerleader on the field.

Mudville got the ball back and kicked the extra point.

The score was tied, seven to seven.

16

It was a close second half, but I'm happy to say OKU squeaked by with a 14-10 victory, and the hundreds of students who crammed into Pappy's Pizza were in a jolly after-game mood.

"I've never been so glad to see the home team win in my life," Jeannie confided as we waited for a table.

"Me, too," Max said. "If we'd lost, the fans would have lynched us from the goal post. Or worse."

The fans, who didn't quite understand about the map, had been pretty perturbed at us for running onto the field during the game. They blamed US when OKU didn't get credit for its touchdown after blocking the Mudville kick.

By now, word had spread that we were trying to capture a criminal moose, and the crowd had mellowed. Some.

The idea of dressing as moose and infiltrating the Mudville mascots hit Supergranny as she, Dreamwhopper and Angela were selling burritos to several hundred antlered Mudville fans before the game.

"I offered one of them $20 to rent his costume and he unzipped it right there at the Burrito Buggy," she said. "Fortunately he had his clothes on underneath."

"Then his friends wanted to rent theirs, too, so the next thing we knew, Professor Dreamwhopper and I were in moose suits," Angela said.

"The Mudville fans even offered to watch Shackleford and Chesterton during the game," Dreamwhopper added. "But of course, the fans couldn't hold them once the action started."

That explained the robot and Old English sheepdog who had passed me on the football field.

"Now that all four moose are behind bars, we can settle down to find those diamonds," Supergranny said.

"At last," agreed Dreamwhopper, pulling the map from his fat briefcase as soon as we were settled at a trestle table with our pizza.

The map was totally crumpled, partly from being hidden behind Dreamwhopper's farmhouse wall for all those years, but mostly because Max had squashed it into a ball to throw to me during the game.

Dreamwhopper smoothed it out the best he could on the middle of our table.

It looked like this:

N

Avenue Elms
From Alpha to
President's Right T

SW 40 Paces

W

E

Behind Boards
Capes of Purple
Crown of Gold
The Queen's Hat
From Days of Old

MDCCCLXXII

S

We all stared at the old piece of paper and chewed pizza.

"It's not much to go on," Angela said.

"Are you sure this is the whole thing?" Vannie asked.

"Are you sure it's real?" Supergranny asked.

I was thinking along those lines myself. How did we know the map wasn't some kind of joke? Maybe a kid had even stashed it there. Maybe old Keptheart's son and a friend had stuck it behind the wall during a remodeling project or something.

"I'm as sure this map is real as I'm sure Leonard is a llama," Dreamwhopper said. "I've checked and cross-checked. Compared the handwriting with Keptheart's old letters. My remodeling contractor assured me the spot where I found the map had been sealed since the late 1800s. A paper expert said the map is on rag paper manufactured in the 1870s."

"Then the date fits," Supergranny said.

She was talking about the Roman numerals in the map's right-hand corner. Those M's and C's and X's. Roman numerals, as you may know, were the most popular numbers around until the 1500s when people started using Arabic numbers (1,2,3,4,5,6,7,8,9 and 0.)

People still use Roman numerals today when they want to be fancy, and they used them even more in the 1800s when Keptheart was kicking.

I learned all about them two years ago in Ms. Hammersmith's class, but I couldn't remember them all. I mean, I can remember X is 10 and I is 1, but D for 500 and L for 50 keep slipping my mind, which is no big deal because I can look it all up under "R" in the encyclopedia anytime I want. Angela, of course, never forgets a Roman numeral or anything else. She translated the date for Vannie and me on a napkin, like this:

M	1,000
D	500
C	100
C	100
C	100
L	50
X	10
X	10
I	1
I	1
MDCCCLXXII	1872

"Right, Angela," Dreamwhopper said. "Max and I think the map was drawn in 1872 when Keptheart was 73. It was a year of big changes in his life. His wife had just died, their son was grown, and he was sad and lonely.

"According to letters written at the time, friends encouraged him to travel. Maybe they thought a change of scenery would cheer him up. It seemed to work. He closed the farmhouse and never lived there again. Too many memories of his wife, perhaps.

"He took a grand tour of Europe. When he came back, he gave the farmhouse to his son and built an elegant house for himself in town. He lived there until he died in 1892. It later burned down."

"We think he may have moved the diamonds to a more secure hiding place before he left on his travels. He probably drew up the map then," Max said.

"But how do you know he didn't move the diamonds later?" Supergranny asked.

"Or sell them? Or maybe he told his son and *he* sold them or something," Angela added.

"We can't be sure," Dreamwhopper answered. "But we don't think so. For one thing, after he took the grand trip to Europe and built his new house, his lifestyle didn't change.

"He lived well, but not lavishly like, say, the Vanderbilts or Astors. No 138-room mansions, yachts, private railroad cars or entertaining royalty at grand balls – which he certainly could have done if he'd sold the diamonds."

"And with $100 million in diamonds he certainly could have out-Vanderbilted the Vanderbilts," Max put it.

"Not to mention out-Astored the Astors," added Jeannie.

"But why?" Angela asked. "If *I* had $100 million worth of diamonds *I'd* certainly build a 138-room mansion with solid gold bathrooms."

"Would you?" Supergranny asked.

We all mulled that over a minute while we chewed pizza.

Actually, deep down, I don't even *want* a 138-room mansion with gold bathrooms. It might be lonely and every place would be too far from the kitchen and I'd forget where I put stuff and people might be jealous and just play up to me because of my palatial mansion.

Maybe Caleb didn't either. Maybe he liked the house he had. Maybe he liked that everybody in Keptheart, Ohio, thought he was a wonderful guy and that if he sold any more of the diamonds, they'd find out about his shady past.

"Actually," Vannie said reaching for another piece of taco pizza, "I'd rather have a house like Super-granny's – especially the secret room behind the fireplace."

"Secret room?" Dreamwhopper asked.

"You have a secret room behind your fireplace?" Jeannie asked.

Vannie dropped her pizza and looked at Supergranny, her mouth making an upside-down smile.

We are never, never, never supposed to mention Supergranny's secret room without her permission. That's *her* territory. If she wants people to know, *she* tells them. After all, Max, her own nephew, hadn't even told them.

"I'm sorry," Vannie said in the weak, squeaky voice she uses when she's in trouble and trying to make everyone feel sorry for her.

Supergranny laughed. "Never mind, Vannie. I was going to tell Delano and Jeannie anyway and invite them to come out with Max to visit. In fact, I thought my office-workshop-laboratory-playroom-garage would be a great place for the engagement party."

Now Angela and I dropped our pizza.

What engagement party? Who was getting engaged??

85

We were stunned. Supergranny had just met
Dreamwhopper the day before. I knew she liked him;
we all liked him. But surely they weren't engaged!
Wasn't that rushing things??

Unhappy thoughts jammed together in my brain.

Would Supergranny move away?

Would she stop fighting crime?

Would we stop having adventures together?

But wait – Max was talking. And he had a big grin
on his face.

I tried to unjam my brain enough to listen.

"Jeannie and I have a surprise for you," he was
saying. "Aunt Sadie has known for a month, but she's
kept our secret. As you know, we'll both be
graduating in June. We plan to work for most of the

summer to save money, then get married in August."

Angela, Vannie and I sighed in relief.

*Max and Jeannie were the ones engaged!!
Hooray!!!*

We'd never been so happy about an engagement in our lives. We jumped up and hugged Max and Jeannie while Dreamwhopper toasted them with his iced tea and said he couldn't wait to come to Illinois for the engagement party and to see Supergranny's secret room behind the fireplace.

Then we got back to business.

Where were the diamonds?

Supergranny passed out pencils and papers from her purse and suggested we each copy the map's instructions.

"Concentrate," she ordered. "Let's take it from the top – *Avenue Elm,*" she said. "Is there an Avenue Elm in Keptheart?"

"That's just the problem, Aunt Sadie," Max said. "There's an Oak Street, Buckeye Drive and Fern Court – but no Elm."

"Not now, maybe, but how about in 1872?" Angela asked. "Street names change."

"That's another problem," Dreamwhopper said, pulling a massive "History of Ohio Keptheart University" from his fat briefcase. It had a great picture of the campus on the cover. There were horses and buggies in the street and students wearing old-fashioned clothes walking along a tree-lined path to Keptheart Hall.

Dreamwhopper flipped quickly to an old "Plat of Keptheart."

"No Elm Avenue, don't you see?" he said, running his finger down a street index.

We stared at the street map and concentrated again.

"Maybe its MLE spelled backward," Vannie suggested. "Is there a MLE Street?"

"MLE Street?" I said. "*MLE Street??*"

"I know it sounds weird, but it could be somebody's name," she said. "Maybe there was a settler from Moravia or somewhere who had a name like that, and they named a street after her or something ...," she said.

Dreamwhopper checked the street index to make her happy.

No MLE.

"I think I've got it," Supergranny said. "Let's take another look at that book's cover."

There it was, staring us in the face.

"*The trees!*" We shouted together.

"*They're like an avenue,*" Angela said.

"*They're elms!*" Dreamwhopper said. "At least they were. Unfortunately, the elm blight killed them, so they're not there anymore."

"That's where the map starts," Supergranny said. "It must, because the next words are '*From Alpha,*' which is, of course, the first word of –"

"– the Greek alphabet," Dreamwhopper finished.

"And it's often used to mean 'beginning'," Angela said. "As in the hymn, 'From Alpha to Omega,' or, 'from beginning to end'."

We made quick restroom pit stops, grabbed our jackets and took off for the main campus ... for the spot where the line of elms *used* to begin.

"Alpha to Omega," Angela repeated excitedly. "From

beginning to end."

Except it wasn't "Alpha to Omega." It was "Alpha to President's Right T."

What ... or where ... was "President's Right T?"

*   *   *   *

By now it was dark and we were working by flashlight.

There had been ten trees, spaced about fifteen feet apart, on each side of the walk. From looking at the picture, we could pick out where the first trees had stood.

"Now all we have to do is start where the first tree was and go to President's Right T," Jeannie said. "But what's that?"

Nobody knew.

We were stumped, a bad pun but true.

What in heck was "President's Right T"?

We sat down on the campus wall and brainstormed about "T": 'T' intersection? (treasure buried in a road near the university president's house?); Golf tee? (treasure hidden in a hole on a golf course??); Cup of tea? (treasure hidden in president's tea pot???)

"By the way," Supergranny asked. "Who was the University president in 1872?"

"I believe it was Elijah O. Price," Dreamwhopper said, whipping out his "History of Ohio Keptheart University" again. "Yes, don't you see, right here."

He held the book up with his flashlight on the president's picture. Old Elijah O. Price had bristly white hair, full sideburns and mustache and a neatly trimmed beard. He was wearing a dark suit and polka-dot tie and if he knew where $100 million in diamonds were stashed, he wasn't talking. Supergranny sighed. "That shoots

89

down my idea. I thought perhaps there might be a 'T' in his name. Say, the third letter or something. Then we'd know the map meant, 'Go to the third Tree.'"

"Good idea, Sadie," Dreamwhopper said.

"Yes, the simplicity fits," Max said.

"Just start at the first tree and go to the third one," Jeannie said.

"Except there's no 'T' in 'Price,'" Angela said.

"Or 'Elijah,'" I said.

"Or 'O,'" Vannie said.

It hit us all at once.

"WAIT A MINUTE! MAYBE IT DOESN'T MEAN THE *UNIVERSITY* PRESIDENT!" about six people shouted.

"MAYBE IT MEANS THE U.S. PRESIDENT!" seven people shouted.

Personally, I was stumped again because I didn't know who was president of the United States in 1872. That's another little bit of data like Roman numerals that I don't carry around in my head. When I need it, I look in the encyclopedia under "P".

Nobody happened to have Volume P on him, but it didn't matter, because Dreamwhopper, Max, Jeannie, Supergranny and Angela *all* carry the U.S. presidents and their terms of office around in their heads. I guess they want to be prepared for an emergency.

"GRANT!" they shouted. "ULYSSES S. GRANT! EIGHTEENTH PRESIDENT OF THE UNITED STATES! SERVED FROM 1869 TO 1877!"

We galloped back to "alpha", the spot where the first tree had stood on the right side of the path. We figured it to be the *right* side of the path, since Keptheart had written "President's *right* T."

We figured the first tree was "G." We raced past the second tree (R), the third tree (A) and the fourth tree (N) to THE FIFTH TREE (T)!

"What's next? What'snextwhat'snextwhat'snext??" Dreamwhopper asked, getting so excited he forgot the rest of the map's directions.

"SW 40 paces," Supergranny read.

"Obviously, it means 'southwest,'" Angela put in.

Dreamwhopper was way ahead of her. He already had his compass out and was pacing across campus in the dark, just a few steps behind Supergranny.

Forty paces took us up the steps, right to the front door of the math building.

"He hid one hundred million dollars' worth of diamonds in the *math* building?" Angela asked.

"Weird," Vannie said.

Dreamwhopper stood there shaking his head. Just stared at the old math building door and shook his head, then turned and faced us sadly.

"It's no use," he said. "It's all over. The building that stood here in Keptheart's day was torn down long ago. It was the old campus theater, and it was replaced by the math building in the early '30s. If the diamonds were hidden there, they're gone forever. It's no use, my friends. We're whipped."

The 1844 room of the Student Center was deserted except for a bearded guy playing "The Warsaw Concerto" on a grand piano. The center is a humongous building with a dance hall, coffee shop and bowling alley downstairs and two giant living rooms on the main floor.

The living room on the left is called the 1844 Room, because that's the year the university was founded, and the furniture is typical 1844 furniture except that the lamps have real electric bulbs instead of kerosene.

The one on the right is the 1954 Room, because that's the year the Center was built, and the furniture is typical 1954 except that the TV is a giant 60-inch-screen model instead of a little black-and-white one like most people had back then. It was full of people watching an old "Night of the Living Dead" movie.

We picked the 1844 so we could enjoy our misery in peace and quiet except for "The Warsaw Concerto."

Dreamwhopper slouched in a wingback chair and scowled, his long legs stretched out in front of him. Shackleford sat on the floor beside him. She kept nuzzling his arm to try to cheer him up, but he just scratched behind her ears absently and scowled some more.

Supergranny sat on what they call a horsehair sofa with Chesterton on her lap. She was making notes on a clipboard. Every now and then she'd stop and stare at the piano player, but she didn't seem to see him.

The rest of us sat at a pretty wooden table with a dark green leather top. We were playing Skip-bo to take our minds off how we'd been about sixty years too late to find the diamonds.

"If we'd only found the map before the old theater building was torn down in 1934," Jeannie said.

"Of course, we weren't *born* in 1934," Max pointed out.

"I just feel so sorry for the professor," Angela whispered. "He worked so hard to find those diamonds."

Suddenly, Supergranny's voice sliced through the gloom and doom and "Warsaw Concerto."

"Theater building. Boards. Capes of purple. Crowns of gold," she was saying, her brow knit in thought. "Theater building. Boards. Theater building. Capes of purple. Theater building. Crowns of gold."

93

"DELANO!" she yelled, jumping up so fast Chesterton crashed to the carpet. "I've got it! Maybe 'behind boards' doesn't mean the diamonds were hidden in the walls of the old building. 'Boards' also is another word for stage. Maybe the map meant the diamonds were *behind stage!*"

It made sense, but it didn't do a lot for Dreamwhopper's funk. "They're still gone, Sadie," he said sadly. "Backstage is gone, too. Torn down. Demolished."

"But maybe the diamonds were saved," Supergranny said, "When you tear down a building you don't throw out everything in it. You might save the furniture."

"Or the scenery," Angela said.

"Or the costumes," Max added, his voice shaking.

"Capes of purple ... crowns of gold," Jeannie said slowly.

"The queen's hat from days of old!" Supergranny finished. "DELANO, YOUR HISTORY BOOK! QUICK!!"

Dreamwhopper fished it out of his briefcase and tossed it to her.

She slammed it down on our Skip-bo table and turned quickly to the Ks in the index. Her finger slid right past "Keptheart, Caleb," and landed on "Keptheart, Queen Anne, thespian, page 47."

"Queen Anne, what?" Vannie asked.

"Thespian," Angela said, her voice starting to shake, too. "It means actor or actress. I think I'm catching on ...."

Great, everybody was catching on but

Dreamwhopper and me.

"Yes, of course, Keptheart's wife was an actress. She retired from the *professional* stage when she married, but she was a great patron of *amateur* theater and even appeared in many plays herself," Dreamwhopper said. "And her name was 'Queen Anne' — LIKE ON THE MAP!"

Great. Dreamwhopper was catching on. Everybody but me was catching on.

"WOW," I said, feeling like a numskull.

"And she played a queen on stage!" Supergranny pointed to a picture of Keptheart's wife all decked out in a long robe and wearing a crown. A familiar crown. A crown I'd seen somewhere before.

"My tiara!" Jeannie gasped. "She's wearing the tiara I wore in the Comedy Club last night. I found it in a trunk in the theater department with some old costumes ... you mean, the diamonds in my tiara are *real*?"

It was such a shock I thought she was going to faint, but she didn't. Unfortunately, Max did, kablonk, right on the floor, just missing the edge of the Skip-bo table. Vannie ran to the restroom for a wet paper towel and Jeannie went down to the coffee shop for a cup of water.

In the excitement, it was several minutes before Supergranny had a chance to ask Jeannie the hundred-million-dollar question: "Jeannie, dear, where is the tiara now?"

"In the costume room in the basement of the theater building; I always — Wait! No, it's not. I didn't have time to go down there after my act."

She stopped, her face a panicked blank.

"Right!" Angela said. "We were so worried about Supergranny and Professor Dreamwhopper...."

"Right!" Max said. "I got the Ferrari and pulled it up to the alley...."

"Right!" Vannie said. "We left in a hurry because we were worried about Supergranny."

"But where did you *put* the tiara," Max asked, a trifle testy.

"Well, I — $100 million," Jeannie groaned, so panicked her eyeballs locked. "I can't have lost a $100-million tiara. But where is it? I can't think."

Supergranny put her arm around Jeannie and laughed. "Calm down, honey. Just sit beside me on the horsehair loveseat and rerun what you did last night through your mind."

She glanced at the rest of us: "All of you, start with the end of Jeannie's act and *think* what happened. Every little detail."

I tried to start thinking at the end of the act, but my mind insisted on starting with us driving the Ferrari through the fog instead, so I had to work backwards.

Before that, Max and I had picked up Jeannie, Angela and Vannie at the alley door. Before that — a slam.

There was a slam. I remembered hearing a slam.

It was the trunk. *Jeannie hadn't had time to take her costume back to the theater department. She'd put it in the trunk of the Ferrari.*

"The Ferrari," I gasped. *"There are 100 million dollars worth of diamonds in the trunk of Supergranny's Ferrari!"*

Dreamwhopper, Max and Jeannie drove out to Illinois several weeks later for the engagement party. They pulled Leonard along behind in a horse trailer.

The regular party guests would use the garage door to Supergranny's workshop-office-laboratory-playroom-garage. Supergranny likes to keep the fireplace doors *we* use secret for security reasons.

Of course, Max, being Supergranny's nephew, had known about Supergranny's secret entrance for years. In fact, he'd played in the office when he was a kid, way back in the years when Supergranny drove a Corvette instead of a Ferrari. It's old stuff to him.

But the office was a surprise to Jeannie, Dreamwhopper and Leonard. They knew she *had* one, of course, because Vannie had let it slip at

Pappy's Pizza.   But they didn't dream how equipped it was.

We gathered in Supergranny's kitchen before the party. Vannie passed around snickerdoodle cookies with the secret ingredient, and we all lined up in front of the fireplace, which has benches on each side and a yellow button just inside the hearth.

As you may know by now, to make the fireplace doors spring open, you first eat a snickerdoodle with the secret ingredient, then push the yellow button.

Leonard gummed his snickerdoodle around a while, but finally swallowed it.

"And now, Jeannie, my future niece-in-law, please do the honors and push the yellow button," Supergranny requested.

Jeannie pushed it.

Instantly, the fireplace sprang open in the center, and "Stars and Stripes Forever" boomed from the ceiling.

Leonard jumped a foot. He was so surprised, I was afraid we might have a llama stampede right there in the kitchen, but Shackleford and Chesterton saved us. They barked and beeped at his rear heels until they herded him through the open fireplace doors into the office. The rest of us ducked inside, and the sliding doors closed behind us.

Jeannie and Dreamwhopper were astounded.

I can't blame them. The first time I saw the office, I thought it was the best room in the world. I thought you could live for 137 years and never see a better one. I still do.

Jeannie kept saying things like, "Fascinating.

Amazing. Unique. UN-BE-LIEV-A-BLE."

Dreamwhopper kept saying things like, "I've seen everything from the Inca ruins at Machu Picchu, Peru, to the underground clay army in China but I've NEVER seen anything like this."

They liked the vending machine balcony that has about anything you want in the way of food–pineapple pizza, coconut cream pie, ribs – just push a button, no money required. But their favorite part of the room was the southeast corner.

It's set off from the rest of the room by a white picket fence and gate.

Directions are posted on the fence:

1. Lock the gate.
2. Push the button beside the activity you want.

There is a long list of activities with buttons beside them mounted along one side of the fence. "Basketball Court," "Hot Tub," "Helicopter Pad" and "Swimming Pool," for example.

Jeannie pushed the button marked "Hot Tub."

Before you could say "Queen Anne Keptheart," a yellow-and-white curtain fell and rose again.

And there on the other side of the fence was a steamy hot tub complete with a stack of red, white and blue beach towels.

It had hardly appeared when Dreamwhopper pushed "Basketball Court."

Before you could say "Forever Gold," the curtain fell and rose again to reveal a regulation basketball court and half a dozen basketballs.

They were still pushing buttons when the garage doorbell rang. The first guest had arrived.

20

All Supergranny's old friends, including Mom and Dad, showed up for the party. They were eager to congratulate Max, meet Jeannie, and hear all about the $100-million diamond caper. But mostly they were eager to meet Dreamwhopper, because word had spread that Supergranny had a gentleman friend.

Some of them seemed a little surprised to see he had brought a llama, but they took it well. "Shows he isn't stuffy," Captain Tubweathers[1] whispered to Mom and me.

Leonard did look especially nice with a big green-and-white bow fastened to his collar.

---

1. More about Captain Tubweathers in *Supergranny 2: The Case of the Riverboat Riverbelle.*

The green-and-white bow was in honor of OKU. After we found the diamond tiara in the trunk of the Ferrari, Dreamwhopper had turned it in for the one-million-dollar reward and given it *all* to OKU for scholarships. Thanks to him, thousands of students who could not have afforded college otherwise would get an education at OKU.

Jeannie and Max stood near the door, shaking everybody's hand and laughing whenever someone told them what a great-looking couple they were.

After the refreshments, everybody settled down to hear a recap of the case.

"Sadie, I insist you tell us about those diamonds," Myrtle Richmont[2] said. "I've always been fond of diamonds."

"Did you bring back samples for your friends?" joked Boots[3], Mom's cousin from West Virginia.

"I want to hear about those wacky moose," said Meg,[4] Max's sister, who had flown in from Germany for the party.

"And who was Mysterious Hooded Sweatshirt?" asked Professor Picklesnip.[5]

"OK, OK, OK, " Supergranny said, laughing as she settled Chesterton on her lap. "Do you want the long version or a three-in-one?"

---

2. More about Myrtle Richmont in *Supergranny 1: The Mystery of the Shrunken Heads.*

3. More about Boots in *Supergranny 4: The Secret of Devil Mountain.*

4. More about Meg, Supergranny's great-niece, in *Supergranny 3: The Ghost of Heidelberg Castle.*

5. More about Professor Picklesnip in *Supergranny 1: The Mystery of the Shrunken Heads.*

"How long is the long version?" asked world-famous mystery writer Victoria Charmain, who'd flown in for the party from Chicago with her sister, Olivia.[6]

"About three hours," Supergranny answered.

"We'll take the three-in-one," Olivia said quickly.

Everybody laughed.

A three-in-one, as you may know, is a summary done in three sentences in only one minute. Supergranny invented it to help Angela boil down her reports. Otherwise, Angela would talk for years. Once she got an A+ on a report about President Franklin D. Roosevelt and was DETERMINED to tell Vannie and me the whole thing.

She started the day school was out and nearly ruined our summer vacation. By the Fourth of July, Vannie and I were so desperate we gave her my last five dollars and Vannie's Whitney Houston tapes to get her to stop.

"Angela," Supergranny asked, "how about a three-in-one recap of the case?"

Angela, who loooooves to give reports, was delighted.

Supergranny tossed me her stopwatch, and I gave Angela a minute to organize her thoughts, then started the countdown:

"Ten, nine, eight, seven, six, five, four, three, two, one, GO!"

She was off:

"In 1819 a young English sailor jumped ship in

---

6. More about Victoria and Olivia Charmain in *Supergranny 5: The Character Who Came to Life.*

Bombay, India, after swiping fabulous diamonds from thieves who had stolen them years before and, fearing jail, changed his name to Caleb Keptheart and finally settled in Ohio where he married a former actress, founded OKU, sold some of the diamonds, then hid the rest in a tiara for his wife to wear onstage, a clever hiding place because the diamonds looked too big and gaudy to be real."

"Twenty seconds," I said.

"After Professor Dreamwhopper bought Caleb's farmhouse he discovered a mysterious map and papers linking Caleb to the diamonds, so he and Max began researching Caleb, but Rex, a student flunking the professor's history class, broke into Max's computer looking for test answers, stumbled onto information about the diamonds, then dropped out of college and recruited three thugs for his gang."

"Forty seconds," I said.

"Following two botched breakins at the farm, Rex and gang returned on Homecoming weekend dressed as moose to blend in with the Mudville Moose fans, and Rex, wearing a hooded sweatshirt, sneaked into Max's room for a diamond update, then captured Supergranny and Dreamwhopper, who fooled him with a phony map, but Rex, who the others called "Main Moose," didn't return to the farmhouse with the gang; instead he hid, then followed us back to campus and watched from the shadows as we gave away the secret that the map was hidden in Caleb's statue; however, we beat him to the map during the Homecoming game and then discovered the diamonds were in the very tiara Jeannie wore in her Comedy Club act!"

"TIME!" I yelled.

Everybody cheered and applauded and begged Jeannie to do her Comedy Club act for them.

At first she modestly refused, but they begged and insisted some more, so we called up the costume room in the southeast corner. Angela and Vannie found Jeannie a purple satin dress and some hiking boots while I went home for Shackleford's pooper scooper. There didn't happen to be a $100-million diamond tiara in Supergranny's costume room, so Mom and Dad made Jeannie a tiara from cardboard and aluminum foil and we pinned costume jewelry on it.

"It's beautiful," Vannie told Mom and Dad.

"It's almost as gaudy as the real diamond tiara," Angela said.

"I think I like it better," I said.

Dreamwhopper pushed the "Little Art Deco Theater" button on the fence in Supergranny's southeast corner, and the yellow curtain fell, then rose again.

Before us was a small, old-fashioned theater with a scarlet, velvet curtain and curved, dark green walls with shiny chrome trim.

All the guests took seats out front while Supergranny went backstage with Jeannie.

The lights dimmed. Music played. The spotlight shone. The curtain parted.

Jeannie stood center stage wearing a purple satin dress and an aluminum foil tiara that glittered like diamonds.

She looked beautiful and elegant, except she was also wearing hiking boots and carrying a megaphone and pooper scooper.

Everybody laughed as she clomped to the front of the stage to lead her totally ritzy, dog-obedience class.

Once again, she introduced her imaginary dogs, Dinky, Suds, Bartholomew and Chuck.

I thought the college audience had gone wild at her act, but it was nothing compared to this. People chased imaginary dogs and laughed and clapped and hugged and cheered ... delighted that Jeannie had come into their lives, along with Dreamwhopper and Max and Supergranny and each other.

Not to be left out, of course, Shackleford, Chesterton and Leonard raced around the room barking and beeping and humming, until — just in the nick of time — we remembered what Leonard meant when he hummed.

ABOUT THE AUTHOR

Beverly Van Hook grew up in Huntington, West Virginia, graduated from Ohio University, Athens, and now lives in Rock Island, Illinois. A journalist who wrote for national magazines before turning to fiction, she has received numerous writing awards, including the Cornelia Meigs Award for Children's Literature and the Isabel Bloom Award for the Arts. She is married to an advertising executive and has three children and an Old English sheepdog exactly like Shackleford.

ABOUT THE ARTIST

Catherine Wayson grew up in Iowa and now lives in Huntsville, Alabama, where she is a full-time professional illustrator and free-lance artist and photographer. Her paintings and photographs have appeared in juried shows nationally and throughout the Midwest.